GONE BEFORE
THE MOON
WILLIAM LEE

ISBN: 9798311271165

This is a work of fiction. Any similarities to actual persons, living or dead, or real events are purely coincidental.

Beta read by: @alyxreads (Fiverr)

Proofread by: Alex Adie and Emily-May Sandalls

Cover Formatting by: Joshua Carter

THE TRUTH IS BURIED
ONLY THE BOLD DARE TO DIG

PROLOGUE

The metallic tang of blood and antiseptic hung heavy in the air as she stumbled through the narrow corridor, her breath ragged and uneven. Fluorescent lights flickered above, casting jagged shadows that seemed to chase her every step. Her red headband was soaked with sweat, a few strands of her dark hair plastered to her face. Her hands trembled as she gripped the edges of the dark coat she'd stolen, the oversized fabric billowing behind her like a ghost.

Run.

The voice wasn't hers. It never was.

They're coming.

Others chimed in, a cacophony of whispers and shouts that made her skull throb. She clenched her teeth, trying to drown them out, but it was no use. They were always there, an endless crowd in her mind, arguing, screaming, begging.

She turned a corner, her bare feet slapping against the cold tile, and froze. The room ahead was small and dark, except for the faint green glow of a monitor in the corner. A figure lay sprawled on the floor, half-hidden by shadows. Her heart lurched as recognition slammed into her.

"Billy," she whispered, her voice barely audible over the pounding in her ears.

Her brother's lifeless eyes stared back at her, unblinking. His body was contorted, twisted as if he'd fought

1

until the very end. She dropped to her knees beside him, her fingers brushing against his bloodied cheek. He was still warm.

He's gone.

You can't save him.

Leave him.

"No," she hissed, shaking her head. The voices swirled, growing louder, overlapping until she could barely think. Tears blurred her vision as she gripped his shirt, shaking him gently, then harder.

"Billy, wake up," she pleaded. Her voice cracked, and the words broke into a sob.

They'll catch you.

Elena, you need to go.

A distant alarm blared, its sharp wail snapping her back to reality. The pounding of boots echoed from somewhere down the hall, growing louder with every second.

Her body moved before her mind could catch up, instincts driving her forward. She pressed a trembling kiss to Billy's forehead, then forced herself to stand.

"I'm sorry," she whispered, her voice breaking. With one last glance at her brother's lifeless form, she turned and bolted.

The halls twisted and turned in ways that made no sense, but she didn't stop. The voices screamed warnings, guiding her through the maze of corridors. Her bare feet skidded around a corner, and she crashed into a steel door. Locked.

"No, no, no," she muttered, fumbling with the keypad beside it. Numbers flooded her mind, fragments of codes she'd seen in passing. Her fingers moved on their own, tapping in a sequence before she even realised what she was doing.

The lock clicked. The door groaned open, and she stumbled outside into the night. The cold air hit her like a slap, sharp and biting against her damp skin. She sucked in a deep breath, the scent of pine and earth replacing the sterile stench of the lab. For a moment, the voices in her head quieted, like they were catching their breath too.

But there was no relief. Not yet. She glanced back at the facility, its harsh lights glowing faintly through the trees. Somewhere inside, the doctor would be searching for her. He wouldn't stop. Not until he dragged her back, kicking and screaming, to finish what he'd started.

Her fingers brushed against her headband, the only thing left of the woman she used to be. She tightened it and stepped into the shadows of the forest, her body trembling with grief and fury.

Billy was gone... But she wasn't... Not yet...

ONE
Kade

Dad,

I pray this letter reaches you. By now Mum has probably told you about what I've done. Believe me, it's not true. She has gotten it all wrong.

The night Billy went missing wasn't an accident, it also wasn't my fault. We were taken. It's that guy again. The doctor. The one that I said kept staring at me through the window.

I know I should have told you the truth sooner but I couldn't bear to see the fear in your eyes when you found out. If he finds out I'm still alive I'm a dead woman. I fear he will do anything to find me. It's not safe for me to be around you so I have left London. I can't say where I am now, but I can only hope this letter finds you.

Forgive me for everything.

Love you always.

- ***Unknown Letter — Friday, 11th April 2025***

The shrill sound of the alarm slices through the stillness of the early morning, dragging me from a restless sleep. My eyes snap open, heart racing as I realise how late I am. The morning light filters through the blinds, too bright for someone who's barely slept. I briefly stare at the cracked ceiling of Duncan's guest room, a world away from home. If you can even call it home anymore. Duncan's house is warm, inviting, but it'll never feel like mine. Not without Mum's laughter from the kitchen or Dad's terrible puns filling the silence. Here, the silence feels permanent. My parents died in a car crash a few months ago. A drunk driver is the cause of my pain and loss inside.

The minutes have slipped away unnoticed, and now I'm in a frantic scramble. When I woke up, it was from the latest out of the five alarms I'd set for the morning. I wasn't planning on waking up when this rang, as it was set for when I was supposed to leave. It was sort of set up as a last-ditch effort if I couldn't manage to slumber my lazy body out of bed the first four times.

Sheets tangled around my body, I fumble for my phone, swiping it in a blur. The clock on the wall seems to mock me as I dash from room to room, the familiar chaos of a hurried morning settling in.

As I pass the bathroom I barely spare a glance at the bathroom mirror, skipping the usual brush of my teeth as I rush through the motions. My Nike Air forces are nowhere in sight, so I grab the nearest pair of trainers I can find. They are ones that don't even fit right, but it hardly matters now. I am in a rush against time to catch the bus, to where I am going to meet my friends Aaron and Joe at Rampage Arena. This wasn't even close to being as cool as it sounded, in fact nowhere near. The Rampage Arena to some is simply an abandoned skate park that people smoke and drink at; but for me, it isn't just an escape, it's the only place where I feel like myself. Or at least, what is left of me.

Duncan is already at the door, keys in hand. He's dressed like he always is; neat, put-together, like he actually cares. His blonde hair is carefully styled, not a strand out of place. Meanwhile, I look like I lost a fight with my bedsheets.

He's clearly had more time to get ready than me, my hair is a mess, looking like a bird's nest on the top of my head. In fact I haven't even dressed well. I'm wearing the same black T-shirt that I had on yesterday. I've covered the body odor stench with a cheap spray-on deodorant that I was given as a stocking-filler last Christmas. A few minutes ago I'd thrown on a pair of baggy looking grey joggers that match the rough, homeless approach I've unintentionally based my look on. Luckily, it's a non-uniform day at school because it's the last day of term, so it won't raise suspicion with Duncan's Mum.

"You look rough," he says with a smirk.

"Didn't have time to be pretty," I mumble, swiping a granola bar from the counter.

"Kade!" Cynthia's voice cuts down the stairs, sharp and exasperated. "You can't keep leaving your mess everywhere. I'm not your maid."

I wince. Duncan sighs. His Mum's usually kind, but ever since she took on extra shifts at work, the stress has worn her thin.

"Sorry! I was just so tired when I got back last night!" I shout back.

Duncan quietly whispers "Ignore my Mum, she's been... tense lately."

I feel sorry for Duncan's mother. She's a really nice lady, as I've known her over all the years, however when too much stress gets on top of someone it brings out the worst in them.

The door clicks shut behind us as we step out onto the damp pavement. The air smells like last night's rain, cool and sharp. Duncan walks beside me, hands in his pockets, his usual thoughtful expression on his face. He never rushes, never fidgets, always thinking.

It's weird, staying at his place. Two months now. Feels

6

longer. Ever since the crash, his Mum, Cynthia, has done everything to make me feel at home. She even got me my own set of keys, like I was just another son. But no matter how much she tries, it's still not home. It never will be.

Duncan glances at me. "You alright?"

"Yeah," I say automatically.

He doesn't push. That's the thing about Duncan, he notices things, but he doesn't always know what to say. He's smart, though. Always has been. He's got this way of seeing things I don't, like he's playing chess while the rest of us are just moving pieces around. He's been like a big brother to me for as long as I can remember. Even when we were kids, he'd try to keep me out of trouble. Not that I always listened. Duncan has always looked out for me, but I've had my moments too.

"Remember Tank?" I ask suddenly, smirking.

Duncan groans. "Unfortunately."

"That guy was a menace. Always stealing lunch money, shoving people around. Then one day, he decided to mess with you." I shake my head at the memory. "Didn't even think, just ran up and swung at him."

"Swung is generous," Duncan says. "More like... flailed."

I snort. "Hey, it worked. Busted his lip."

Duncan smirks but shakes his head. "And earned yourself a trip to the headmaster's office."

"Worth it," I say.

Cynthia wasn't even mad. She just sighed and made us both hot chocolate like nothing had happened. That's how she's always been; quiet, steady, never making a fuss. She's been in my life for as long as Duncan has. Always made sure I had dinner when I was over, slipped birthday presents into my hands like it was nothing. Even now, with everything that's

7

happened, she's trying to hold everything together

As we get to the end of the road I say "See you later, man. Not sure when, depends if I get that haircut."

Duncan just nods, giving a small wave. He has always been a bit quiet and socially awkward, however it's never bothered me, as I like the fact he doesn't bombard me with questions and topics that I would need to talk about.

As Duncan heads left to walk towards the bus stop where the school bus will arrive, I walk in the other direction, towards the bus stop that is on the road adjacent to where we are now. The bus is only minutes away. I pick up the pace, breaking into a light jog.

I turn the sharp corner of the road to see a small dingy bus stop about a hundred yards from where I am. I reach out and grab my phone from my pocket to check the time. I can see my hands slightly shaking because of the frost cold feeling in the air. I see that the time reads *'07:44'* and know that the bus will be there any second.

I pick up the pace again and move into a quicker jog. Before I know it I am sprinting the last few steps to the bus stop. My lungs are burning and the cold air is stinging my throat.

Just as I reach the edge of the curb, the familiar rumble of the engine fills the air. The bus rounds the corner, its headlights cutting through the early morning haze. The brakes hiss as it slows to a stop in front of me, the doors folding open with a metallic clatter. I stand there for a moment, catching my breath, the warmth of the bus's interior is spilling out to meet me as I experience the chill of the street. It feels like a minor miracle that I made it in time, an unspoken harmony between my frantic pace and the bus's impeccable timing.

As I look up at the bus I can't help but glaze over to the bus stop. It's ruined. There's litter scattered over the bench and floor due to the overflowing state of the rusty green rubbish bin. There is also graffiti spray painted on the walls. The phrase *'BEWARE OF THE GOVERNMENT, THEY'RE ALL LIARS'* is written in black; whilst the words *'coward'* and *'TRAITORS'* are also sprayed on, in a cloudy and bubbly font. The scene looks like it should be something out of one of those apocalypse movies, where the world has ended and humanity is only a fraction of what it used to be.

I step onto the light blue bus and feel like I'm about to pass out with how out of breath I've become. I nod to the elderly driver as I pull out my bus pass. The driver seems to take an extra second to inspect it. It feels like his eyes are piercing, looking through me to see if there's any hidden secrets. Almost as if he's scolding me assuming the bus pass would be out of date. I guess my rough look gives off the impression that I'm up to no good. After a few long seconds he eventually gives in and waves me onto the bus.

I squeeze past some of the other passengers. The bus lurches forward and forces me to steady myself on one of the cold metal poles. The aisle is narrow, packed with bodies that shift and sway with each turn. Bags jutter out into my path, and I find myself muttering apologies as I step over a stray foot and brush against someone's shoulder.

The air is thick with a mixture of conversations, the faint hum of the engine, and the tangy smell of damp clothes. Each step seems like a careful negotiation, a dance of avoiding elbows and finding fleeting gaps in the crowd, to inch my way toward the back. I manage to find one seat at the back of the bus next to an old lady with a walking stick. I politely signal to see if the space next to her is free, to which she signals back to show that it was, so I sit.

I put my earphones in and decide to play some of my favourite heavy metal music to keep myself entertained for the journey. Even though the music is loud and sounds as if people are screaming in it, it helps me relax and feel in a calm state. This might be due to my recent stresses in life. Everything has gone against me so the screaming music seems to represent what's going on inside my head and soothes me.

After around twenty minutes of the rather unpleasant journey bumping across various potholes and swerving round traffic and corners, the bus arrives in a less facilitated area of the city. It's the outskirts where not much other than some trees and the occasional car seem to appear. Only about a twenty minute walk to the skatepark.

I make my way off the now less crowded bus, walking with far more ease down the middle aisle. It seems so much more roomy now that the commuters have all gotten off.

I hop off the bus in good spirits and take a second to take in the scenery. The cold fresh air hits me again like a brick and sends a shiver down me. As I look, I can see that there's a lot of foliage by the side of the road. It is really 'In the sticks' as they say. I can hear the faint chirps of birds that are hiding in the nearby trees, waiting for the right time to go out and get some food.

I begin my walk down the long country road with a spring in my step knowing that I'm not far from relieving stress with my friends with the help of some drinks and smokes.

Even though I'm on my way to meet friends at the skatepark I don't actually skate myself. I merely enjoy watching my friends do it and hanging out with them. The metallic clattering sound of the trucks hitting the grinding rail, and the rolling sound of the wheels on the floor seems to be almost therapeutic. This has become an even bigger habit the past two months since my parents passed.

I open my black rucksack to reveal a bottle of off brand Russian vodka and a packet of cigarettes. I decided to take the vodka out and have a small swig of it, the taste hitting the back of my throat like a bullet, making me pull a face that you would if eating something sour.

In the distance I can see the bus going out of sight, probably going to loop back around to the next town and head back. It's always been a weird habit of mine to try and figure out where buses were going, even if I wasn't on them. Sometimes I think I'm a bit too nosey and into other peoples business.

I've still got my music blasting in my ears which seems to give me a bit of swagger in my walk. It almost makes it look as if I'm dancing as I'm walking up the isolated road, Salsa-ing my way to the skatepark.

The cold chill in the air seems as though it is starting to clear up. I think to myself, 'maybe we're in for the hottest day of the year so far,' not that it would be an achievement. It seems to have been colder than ever this year, but maybe this will be the turning point.

I tug my phone from my pocket, my fingers stiff from the chill. A song I hate comes on. It's one of those indie bands trying too hard to be heavy metal. I sigh, my thumb hovering over the screen to skip it.

A sudden screech of tires shreds through the music. My head snaps up. Too late. A blur of metal. The roar of an engine. A crushing impact.

Pain explodes through me, stealing the air from my lungs. My body is weightless for a split second before I collide with something hard. The world spins, the ground rushing up to meet me. Distantly, I hear footsteps. Heavy. Approaching.

I fight to keep my eyes open, but darkness pulls me under.

TWO
Duncan

I hop off the old run down school bus and set sights on the school gates. As I look back I am shocked by the poor maintenance of the vehicle. The smell of fumes coming from the probably broken exhaust fills the air. I think to myself 'What a brilliant thing for young teenagers to be breathing in.' The dark gas coming from the exhaust makes me heave. It almost looks like something out of a war movie.

I walk down the side of the bus and notice my reflection in the window. My blue eyes look tired, probably from staying up too late again, and a few freckles dot the bridge of my nose. I hate them. I'm not one of the lucky ones like Kade who gets clear skin. I run a hand through my blonde hair, making sure it's still neat, using the window as a mirror. I've always kept it tidy, like somehow that makes everything else feel less chaotic. Chaos isn't something I enjoy as I always try to think one step ahead and keep things in order. I can't help but notice that my frame looks even skinnier in the faint, warped glass. Great, another reminder that I look like I'd get knocked over by a strong breeze.

As I make my way through the school day, nothing out of the ordinary seems to occur. Everyone seems to be in a good mood. It seems as if everyone could already feel the holiday break waiting just around the corner. As I was passing through the corridors earlier I heard chatter from multiple students asking what their plans were for the small amount of time off we would be getting. It seems to help the day go quicker.

It's lunch time now and as I'm walking to the canteen, I am already imagining the sausage rolls and cakes waiting for me. Mr. Stanley steps out from a doorway, his tall frame almost blocking my path. His short black hair is combed neatly, and his glasses catch the fluorescent light above us. He's my head of year and usually only pulls students up when there is something wrong.

"Duncan," he says, his tone polite but firm.

I stop in my tracks, suppressing a groan. Couldn't this wait until after lunch? The smell of freshly baked food drifts out of the canteen, teasing me.

"Yes, sir?" I reply, trying to sound more interested than I feel.

"Do you know why I want to talk to you?"

I shake my head, feigning innocence, though I can already guess where this is heading.

"It's about Kade." He folds his arms, studying my reaction. "He's not in school again today."

My stomach sinks slightly. Kade's habit of skipping school is starting to catch up with us both. "Oh," I say, keeping my face neutral. "He wasn't feeling well this morning."

Mr. Stanley narrows his eyes just a fraction. He's not buying it. "Your Mum said you both walked to the bus stop together. So, what happened after that?"

I hesitate, glancing at the canteen door as if it might somehow save me. Do I lie or tell the truth? I settle on something in between.

"He said he was feeling off, so he probably just went home after the bus, I didn't really think much of it."

Mr. Stanley doesn't respond immediately. Instead, he

13

adjusts his glasses and sighs, the kind of sigh that says I've heard this excuse before.

"Duncan," he says, his tone softer now, "I'm not here to get you into trouble. I just need to know if Kade's okay. He's missed five days this term. That's a pattern. Is there something going on that I should know about? I know he's had his struggle with his parents, but he needs to know that we're here to support him."

I glance down at my shoes, feeling a twinge of guilt. Kade wouldn't want me to spill his secrets, but the concern in Mr. Stanley's voice makes me doubt myself.

"No, sir," I say finally. "He's fine. Really."

Mr. Stanley watches me for another moment, and I can tell he's debating whether to push further.

"Alright," he says eventually. "If you hear from him, let him know he can come to me if he needs anything. And Duncan, if you're covering for him, don't. It won't help him in the long run."

I nod quickly, eager to escape the conversation. "Got it, sir."

"Good. Now go get your lunch before it's all gone."

Relieved, I head into the canteen, but Mr. Stanley's words linger in my mind. Is Kade okay? Usually, I wouldn't worry too much, Kade skips school all the time. But something about today feels different.

I pull out my phone and send him a message. I need to let him know the teachers are getting suspicious. It reads *'Hey mate, Mr Stanley asked where u were, think they're getting onto you, r u ok?'*

With the fact that my Mum is now knowing he's not in school will make this a big problem, she's got enough going on as it is. I know I'm going to get home and just hear her concerned and disappointed lecture.

14

Around twenty minutes pass, nearing the end of lunch, and I still don't have a reply. This is weird as Kade is usually super active on his phone, usually replying annoyingly fast. He probably doesn't have any signal, so maybe I shouldn't worry myself over it.

THREE
Kade

In the shadow of the Eternal Blue Sky, a new breed shall rise. Flesh forged by iron, minds sharpened by the wind of the steppes. Beneath the banner of the Great Khan, the world will bend, not by swords alone, but by the will of those who walk beyond the limits of man. The storm has only begun; the world shall be conquered by those who never tire, never yield.
- **Quote saved on Dr. Magnus Blackthrone's Personal Computer - Genghis Khan, 1220 AD**

My eyelids flicker open, sluggish and heavy. A faint twitch in my fingers pulls me from the void. Life creeps back into my body, slow and unsteady. The first thing I notice is the pain. A dull, throbbing ache that spreads across my body. It is sharp and hot where it shouldn't be. My head feels really heavy, like it has been stuffed with rocks. When I try to move, the world feels like it is tilting violently.

I manage to open my eyes but can't really see anything. The room is dark. A faint metallic tang filling the air, mingling with the acrid stench of burnt rubber and chemicals. I struggle to catch my breathe. I can only breath in short gasps at the moment.

As I look down I appear to be on some sort of hospital bed, this is no hospital however. Even though it is dark I can make out the shadows of several other makeshift beds in the room, with what look like bodies on them. The beds appear to all be made up slightly differently. Through the darkness I can see that some are made up from what look like storage crates with some kind of old tattered blankets draped over the top of them, whilst some look like broken hospital beds. As I look at the bodies on the beds, I wonder if they are also unconscious, or if they're dead. The thought sends a shiver down my spine.

My eyes land on a damaged light switch on the wall to the right of the makeshift bed that I'm on. There seems to be some kind of dark outline on the wall under the switch. The putrid stench coming from it makes me gag. I can only assume that it's made of something like vomit or blood.

I try to sit up, using all of my might to push myself up and out of the bed, but to no avail. My hands brush against something sharp and jagged as I try to move, but I retract them quickly so it doesn't cut me. Shards of glass? Twisted metal? I can't seem to fully make it out, I only see the outline in the suffocating darkness.

The silence is the worst part. It isn't just quiet, it is the kind of silence that presses against your ears, making you hyper-aware of every tiny sound. A faint clink of metal breaks the oppressive silence. My eyes dart down to find a chain locked around my ankle. How had I not felt it? Panic claws at my chest, sharp and unforgiving. How long have I been here? Who did this? The chain seems to be fairly long though so I wonder if I will be able to make my way to the light switch before the chain extends to the limit.

With the room being so quiet, my senses go into overdrive. I think I can make out a distant drip of water echoing through the room, but from where? My pulse thunders in my ears, loud and panicked, as I suddenly realise that I have no idea where I am, or how I got here.

17

I try to piece it together. The crash. It comes back in flashes. Screeching tires, the scream of my body hitting the bonet, the jarring impact that had stolen my breath and plunged me into oblivion. But where am I now? This doesn't feel like the side of the road, or any place familiar. The air is even colder, damp, and oppressive in here, it's clinging to my skin like a shroud.

I need to move, to get out of here, wherever 'here' is. Gritting my teeth against the pain, I push myself to my feet in another attempt to get up, every muscle screaming in protest. My feet are bare, so I subconsciously take small steps, almost scuffing them across the floor, hoping to avoid any glass or debris in my way. My hands reach out, fumbling in the darkness for the switch.

As I slide with my bare feet across the dirty tiled floor, I make my way towards the light switch. I push aside shards of glass with my feet, luckily none of them are cutting me. The chain that connects my ankle to the bed pulls tight as it has been fully extended. I fully stretch out my arm with all my reach, but the switch is just out of touching distance.

I search the nearby surfaces to try and find something I can use to extend my reach. As my hands glide over what I assume are cabinets I accidentally knock over some items. This includes a glass object that smashes when it hits the ground. The sound scatters across the room. I freeze, hoping no one heard that.

After feeling around for a few more seconds I finally manage to get my hands on something. This seems to be a long thin pipe. The coldness of the metal absorbs into my hand in an uncomfortable occurrence. There is a hooked edge on one side. It feels as if it has been crushed by something and bent at almost a right angle. I press the flatter end of the pipe to the switch. It reaches!

18

Suddenly, the lights begin to flicker, before settling into a dim, unsteady glow. There is still a slight flicker from time to time which adds to the creepy and eerie ambiance that the room gives off, but for now, I can see.

The flickering light casts long, shifting shadows, pulling the room into sharper focus. Test tubes are stored next to all the beds, filled with all sorts of coloured liquids. Different documents are scattered across some of the tables. The room reeks of decay and neglect, the kind of place that couldn't exist in any official facility. This is something else; hidden, makeshift, and sinister.

I also look down at the chain that is connecting me to the bed. There appears to be a padlock on it. I start to panic slightly, not knowing how to get it off without a key.

I try to calm myself and focus my eyes. I can see that one of the bodies on the far side of the room is moving slightly. I don't know whether to reach out to them. I'm not sure how to gauge this person. Screw it, if they're in the same mess as me, maybe we can figure a way out together.

"Hey! You okay?" I mutter with a concerned tone, I made it loud enough that they could hear, but not too loud that it might alert whoever put me here.

The person replies back, however it was not with any words that I could make out. Instead it sounds more like a big groan. I'm not sure how to react. I'm glad they've said something, but this wasn't any sort of language I could make out.

"Don't worry, I'm gonna try to get us out of here!" I add tentatively.

I can't make out who the person is, they're laying down and there is some debris in the way, but I'm determined to find out somehow.

There's a small, red, rusty tool box that is propped up

19

on a pile of cardboard boxes to the right of the light switch. Knowing this will be within reach, I force myself to hobble over as close as I can, still avoiding the glass, feeling like I'm doing an obstacle course as I slalom through the shards. I grab the metal bar and use its crushed end to hook around the handle of the toolbox and drag it towards me.

The toolbox crashes to the ground, its rusty contents spilling across the floor with a deafening clatter. I freeze, heart pounding, every nerve in my body screaming to stay still. Did someone hear that?

Kneeling on the cold, gritty floor, I sift through the tools, each breath shallow as I avoid the glass shards glinting nearby. Among the scattered chaos, my eyes catch a hacksaw. My sweaty hands fumble as I grab it, the blade slick with grime. The rancid stench of oil fills the air, turning my stomach.

I saw at the chain desperately, the teeth screeching against the cold, unyielding metal. Each stroke sends vibrations rattling up my arms, my muscles burning. The blade skips; biting, but failing to leave more than faint grooves. The chain mocks me with its stubborn resilience. Minutes stretch into eternity before I slump back, spirit crushed.

COUGH COUGH!

My blood runs cold. "Who's there?" I whisper, my voice trembling.

Behind me, a hulking figure stirs on one of the makeshift beds. He's massive. Easily twice my size. His sharp, calculating eyes seem to pierce through the dim light. His buzz cut and scarred face only add to his intimidating presence. Even lying down, he exudes a quiet menace, and I suddenly feel like prey caught in a predator's gaze.

"Quit it, man. You're driving me nuts. Doc will be back soon," the Brute growls, his voice like gravel. "You don't wanna miss your turn."

My throat tightens. "What do you mean... my turn?" My voice cracks, betraying the terror clawing at my chest. He chuckles, low and guttural, as if savoring my fear.

His words scare me. Doc? My turn? What sort of sick game is this? Am I some kind of lab rat? Maybe this is all in my head and is some kind of sick dream.

I challenge him about what he's said. "What do you mean Doc? And my turn?" I try to speak with confidence but I struggle to get the words out, the stuttering and shaky tone in my voice is a dead give away at how scared I am. It is obvious to him as he lets out another small chuckle.

I hear some footsteps coming from the other side of a bolted door near my bed in the lab and I panic. I rush back, my movements hurried and clumsy. I drag my feet through the glass more carelessly than before. My frantic rushed actions have caused me to misjudge my footsteps, the glass slicing through the soles of my feet like a hot knife through butter. I can't help but let out a small cry. I quickly collapse onto the bed, nearly toppling the bed frame with my speed. I remember waking up on my back, so that's the position I take up. I close my eyes almost all the way as I can't help but want to see who is coming.

The door of the lab creaks open and a slim figure walks through. The bad lighting from the other room almost casts a shadow on his face, so I can't make out too many of his features until he fully steps into the room.

As he walks forward I can see him a bit more clearly. He is clad in a very worn white lab coat. There is a bloodstained handprint near the left breast pocket. I can only imagine what that could have been from. His piercing gaze peers through his thick, round glasses as he searches the room with his eyes, scouring for any abnormalities. I can see that he

21

has a clipboard grasped in one of his hands. I catch a glimpse of it for a second and it appears to be crammed with scribbled notes and diagrams. This gives me the hint of experiments with dubious morality. His short, jet-black hair is slicked back unevenly, receding sharply at the temples, further emphasizing his frantic demeanor. As he's looking around he begins to glance in my direction, I quickly close my eyes, hoping his sharp gaze didn't catch me looking.

With my eyes now closed my biggest asset is my hearing and I'm using it the best I can. I can make out that he is moving through the room, walking over to the brute of a man that I just spoke to. He is muttering under his breath, also sounding like he is scribbling something onto his clipboard. There is a small jingle every time he takes a step, signalling to me that maybe he is carrying the keys to the padlock near my ankle.

"Alright Doc, let's run it then. Don't waste any time." Say the Brute. The Doc doesn't say anything. He seems to be a man of little words.

I can't keep my eyes shut and curiosity gets the best of me. I look to the other side of the room and see that the Doc has a syringe with a bright green liquid inside it. He pulled it out of his pocket, near the bloodstained handprint. The doctor hesitates, he's looking into the Brute's menacing smile. Maybe he's over eager? Or maybe he's got even worse intentions?

After a few seconds he puts it into the Brute's arm and injects it. The Brute doesn't flinch. He turns his head slightly, staring at me directly in my eyes as the needle goes in. The Brute's expression is almost of anger; Intimidation? A warning? What are his intentions?

I realise this may be the best time I can escape. The keys I need are on the doctor however I can't run up to him to grab it. So I have to wait for the right time.

The doctor turns away, his back to the room as he flips through some paperwork on the table. His attention is entirely on the papers in front of him. The quiet hum of the hanging lights fill the space, punctuated only by the faint sound of his shoes scraping against the dirty and stained tiled floor as he moves, absorbed in his work.

Near the small fallen toolbox that housed various tools, a faint glimmer catches my eye. The mallet. Its heavy, worn handle gleams slightly in the dim light, as if it were waiting—waiting for this moment. I'm not sure how I can use it yet. Maybe I can break the chain, maybe I can use it to fight back against the doctor. For now I just need to retrieve it and decide what to do with it later.

My heart is hammering in my chest, each beat louder than the last. My palms are clammy, but I feel as though I have no choice but to make my move now. Slowly, carefully, I swing one leg off the bed, my bare feet brushing against the cold tiles once again. A surge of adrenaline rushes through me, almost haunting me before I even begin. I push through the pain and nerves, and push the dizziness to the back of my mind. I steady myself, taking a breath. Every muscle in my body tenses with the weight of the risk.

My eyes flick back to the doctor. He is still facing the monitors, oblivious in his work. I inch towards the mallet, each step measured and silent. The weight of the moment presses against my chest. My hand hovers over the tool, hesitating, and I quickly grab it, careful not to let it clatter. As I grasp it, the weight of it seems like it could do some damage. It is reassuring, but I can't linger. The doctor is still turned away, but he could turn back at any moment, and the thought of him catching me, of this fragile plan falling apart, makes my heart race even faster.

Inch by inch, I move back towards the bed, my steps

23

deliberate and cautious, each one measured. Every time I make the slightest movement, I freeze, waiting, listening. The seconds stretched on like hours, but the doctor still doesn't seem to notice.

Finally, I am back at the bed, the mallet clutched tightly in my hands, I need to wait for the right moment. I take a quick glance behind me, he is still engrossed in his task. With my heart still pounding in my throat, I settle back down. I tuck the mallet beneath my knee, my hand resting over it to keep it hidden. With no blanket to shield me, I can only pray the doctor doesn't notice the lump beneath my leg.

FOUR
Kade

I lie there, nervously waiting. I can't believe I'm going to attempt this, but I feel as though I have no choice. I have been laying here motionless for about ten minutes and the doctor hasn't moved from the spot. I can hear him shuffling about, but I don't dare to tilt my head back and look.

All of a sudden the footsteps seem to start getting louder and louder, feeling as though I'm in a movie and the music is building up to the action shot. I can still hear the jingle from his pocket and it fills me with excitement.

I slowly move my hand to the handle of the mallet, slow enough that it would not catch the eye of the doctor, unless he is looking directly at it. I can feel a drop of sweat dripping down my face, tickling me as it moves. It stops on the top of my lip and sits there, mocking me, knowing that I can't brush it off.

The footsteps pass me, fading slightly. Now is my chance. I take a deep breath and open my eyes. The doctor is still walking forward, looking straight ahead and doesn't know that I'm getting up.

I'm trying to be as quiet as possible, calculating every move that my body takes. My hands are shaking with nerves. I press them down on the bed, lifting me onto my feet.

KKKRRRRR The sickening crack of a shard of glass

splitting under my foot shoots across the room, piercing my skin as I step on it. I wince in pain. My heart is in my mouth as the doctor stops dead in his tracks. I stop aswell, eyes wide open with shock. I see the doctor spin quickly and go to grab something out of his pocket. Is this it? Is this how it ends?

It's now or never. I lift the mallet, clenching it tightly so that I don't let go. I step forward and swing my arm back. I then swing it forward with all my might and unleash a direct blow. The mallet connects with a sickening thud. The doctor crumbles to the floor, his body limp like a discarded doll. My chest heaves as I stare, adrenaline buzzing through me. Is he dead? Did I... kill him? I can't help but feel like he wasn't normal, the way he was moving before seemed so off.

I shove the thought aside, I don't have time to feel guilt. My hands tremble as I dig into his lab coat. Pens clatter to the floor before my fingers brush cold metal. The keys. I yank them free, their weight in my palm feeling heavier than it should. Hands sweating and shaking, I examine the set. There must be around fifteen different keys on this key chain, all in a variety of different shapes and sizes.

I think to myself, what if he meant for me to take them? How could I come so close to him to grab them? Is this a test? Or did he genuinely not know I was awake.

I flick through the keys, discarding those that clearly don't fit. I rule out the first three as they are far too big for the padlock. They are also more bulky as I am looking for a flat key. I see a key that looks like it could fit. It's greasy and I struggle to get a good grip on it. I'm not sure if this is down to the slippery substance or my shivering hands. I nearly fumble it as I try to put it in the lock, however I get it in. It fits, but it won't turn.

I am panicking, I can't help but get a bit frustrated as I try multiple keys, none of them seeming to work. I flip another key over that looks too big and see one that looks like the perfect fit. I take a deep breath and try again. The key turns smoothly. It works! The chain falls away.

Now that I am free, I don't know what to do. I am in a moral dilemma. Do I run for the exit and escape, or do I turn and see if any of the other people on the beds are alive. They are in the same ruck as me. If they're alive, I can help free them.

This feels like a real head versus heart scenario. I freeze for a second to think. These few seconds feel like an eternity. I start to walk to the door, knowing that I have to get out. I get a few paces from the door, but stop. I think of when my parents were involved in their crash, lying there waiting for help. The incident report I was given stated that they were lying in their car for ten minutes before someone came to help. That ten minutes being the difference between life and death. I take another look back and now know what I need to do. I won't be able to live with myself if I leave these people here to die, or without trying at least.

I turn away from the door and make my way to help the others. I walk up to the Brute, he looks motionless. I know this guy seemed like he wanted to be here, but I have to check. He's not moving so I am a bit confused. I've never really known how to do first aid or anything, but I know I should check for a heart beat. I place two of my fingers to the side of his neck to feel for a pulse, but I don't feel anything. I try to place my hand on his chest to see if I am missing something, but still nothing. I'm in shock. Is he dead? Maybe the injection that the doctor gave him actually killed him?

I search some more of the room, pushing some boxes out the way as I make my way to the next bed. There is a vile stench coming from it. It makes me gag. I put my shirt over my face to try and cover the smell the best I can, but can still feel the disgusting air hitting my nostrils.

There is another body on this bed. I stumble back as there's an older woman in her mid fifties, lying motionless, maggots crawling out of holes that cover her face and throat. I can't look. My hands are shaking. I move away quickly, trying not to throw up. This can't be real. Nobody would leave someone to rot like this.

I head towards the person that made the groan earlier when I called out. As I cautiously approach the body, I can make out that it is another woman based on the body shape and long hair. As I see her, I fall to the ground backwards, landing on my bottom. My hands move quickly to cover my mouth in shock.

"Not another one" I mutter, shredding a tear as the words trickle out my mouth.

I am disgusted and in disbelief at what I see. The woman's face is totally mutilated, worse than the previous. Her throat is almost cut in half, dry blood is everywhere. The Doc must have done all kinds of sick experiments on her, and just left her to rot.

I come to the conclusion that I can't keep checking these bodies. I can't take it. This sick bastard has done all sorts of experiments. Injecting people with unknown liquids that kill them, cutting people open. It's vile.

I make my way back to the door, passing my bed as I get there. My eyes, heavy with pain and confusion, drift to the edge of the hospital bed where a pile of paperwork had been carelessly shoved aside. The sterile white sheets seem to shimmer under the dimness of the lights. I scan the documents, but there, nestled against the metal frame, is something else, something wrong. I can barely make out the jagged, almost prehistoric shapes on the top sheet. Sketches; drawings, not photos. I pick up the pile of papers and look. They appear to be of massive, monstrous wolves, their eyes wild and their fangs bared in a way that suggests more than just the raw power of nature. They were something else entirely. Something... unnatural.

The words underneath the illustrations are blurry at first, my vision swims in and out of focus. But as I blink, the black ink begins to sharpen into legible text: *'Dire Wolf Genetic Reclamation: Incorporating Alpha DNA for Human Enhancement.'*

"What the fuck." I say under my breath.

I look at some more, flicking through the pages. Some text reads *'Methodology for Power Infusion'*, alongside images and diagrams of wires, needles, and broken vials. These were methods I don't want to understand, but feel forced to.

They were going to use this on me? Or have they already started? Knowing with growing horror that I am the next step in whatever twisted ritual this is, I drop the papers. They scatter across the desk and some spew onto the floor. I don't even know if there is anything left of me, any part of me that hasn't already been rewritten. If they've been testing on me already, what's going to happen? Am I going to die? Will I end up like the Brute? Or worse, like the other two women?

I know I have to get out now. What he was planning on doing with me is beyond what I can comprehend.

I am just about to turn and head for the exit when the Brute starts violently shaking, foam oozing out of his mouth. What now? Why another distraction? This is weird, he was dead just seconds ago. Maybe he wasn't dead, maybe they are turning him into something aswell. I can't get distracted. I have to go, and it has to be now.

As I turn back to face the door, the doctor is there, standing strong, his shadow beaming over me. He stands in between me and the door that I need to escape from. I am

29

panicked.

"What the fuck!" I say my thoughts aloud again. How has he recovered so quickly? Most people would have been out cold after that.

I have to make a break for it. I don't have the element of surprise this time, so I have to improvise. I run at him, trying to barge him over, fainting to one side before I hit him. My adrenaline is fueling me to do so. As I attempt to push him out of the way, he moves to the side and uses my momentum to push me into the door. I fall to one knee because of the impact. The doctor is surprisingly nimble for his appearance. Maybe he's enhanced himself with something, or maybe he just used his wit and know-how to dodge out of the way. After all, I didn't exactly disguise my actions that well with the faint.

I am staggered, a little bit dazed, but make my way to my feet. As I turn to face him, some sort of rag is pulled across my face. The stench of chemicals hits me like a train. I try to fight him off, but it's no use. I feel my body fading. I try to keep my eyes open, but it's an uphill battle. I simply can't do it.

Darkness swallows me whole. I don't know if I'll wake up at all, or if I'll wake up as something else.

FIVE
Duncan

The Dire Wolf, A phantom of a wilder past, was more than a predator. It was a symbol of untamed resilience, roaming a world far colder and fiercer than our own.
- ***Quote from Shadows of the lost worlds by Professor Evelyn Harrington, Genetic Evolutionary Studies, 1994***

I jump off the school bus into an unusually busy part of the town. Ravenwood Square is never this loud. The usual hum of traffic and quiet chatter is drowned by angry voices, their shouts bouncing off the statue of Edward Ravenwood. Normally, only the low buzz of a barber's clippers or the scent of Tony's Pizzas drifts through here. Not today. Edward Ravenwood is the only famous person from Hearthwick, my lifelong home. It's a fairly average sized city to be fair. Most big name retailers have shops set up here, but it's also small enough that it doesn't really attract many tourists, or make the news too often.

As I squeeze off the bus into the crowd I can't help but notice the shouting, the signs being held up, and the angry tone of all the people protesting. I assume it's some kind of stand against animal rights or some other controversial topic that I don't want any part of.

31

I slalom through the crowd, careful not to step on anyone's feet, and manage to wiggle my way out. They all seem to be staring at the pizza shop, Tony's Pizzas. I have been to this place before and know the owner quite well. Not to the level that we send each other birthday cards or anything, but he definitely always remembers me when I come in.

I can see the owner, Antonio Bianchi, standing atop the shop. He has a megaphone and looks to be trying to figure out how to work the device.

"LISTEN! These fucking police don't care. It's not just me that's missing someone. Five different cases, YES FIVE. They have gone, without a trace. Taken by someone and we don't have the foggiest who it is. The pigs aren't doing anything. No interviews, no checking cameras, nothing. I think it's time we took this into our own hands. They took my Sophia. She was walking back from seeing her friends and then GONE!" I can see that Antonio is wiping away a tear from his face as he was saying it. What an awful thing to see. Who has taken her? Who else has been taken? Why have they taken her? I'm beginning to get angry.

I can see that Antonio is starting to walk the mob towards the busier side of town; the side that the police station is on. I want to join them, but I know I can't. Kade said he might go for a haircut after he's been with his mate, so I thought I'd do a bit of shopping next door and meet him afterwards.

I glance at my phone and he still hasn't replied to my earlier message about the school questioning where he's been. I suddenly think about Anthonio's rant and wonder if Kade is alright. Surely this isn't connected, he's probably just got no signal. I shake my head. I'm overreacting. Kade's probably just ignoring me... but still. I stare at my phone. One text wouldn't hurt, right? What if they've taken Kade? I can't ask my Mum if he's back, as she'll wonder why we didn't come back together. It's already fortunate that she hasn't been asking about him skipping school.

I can't think of what to text, so I call Kade. No dial tone. Straight to voicemail. My stomach tightens. Kade always texts back, even if it's just a dumb meme or a 'yo.' Silence isn't his thing.

I swallow the lump in my throat and scroll through my contacts, my fingers shaking slightly. Aaron, he was supposed to meet Kade today. He'll know something—he has to. He's usually an honest kid and I know he can't lie for shit.

My fingers start to tremble as I dial the number. The more I think about it, the worse it gets. The phone starts to feel unusually heavy in my hand. I take a deep breath, trying to steady my growing nerves, but my stomach starts to churn with unease. The ringing seems to drag on longer than usual, each ring stretches longer than it should, feeding the anxiety twisting in my chest. I haven't heard from Kade all day, and now, with every unanswered ring from Aaron, a gnawing worry twists inside me.

When Aaron finally picks up, my voice crackles slightly. "Hey, it's… it's Duncan. Uh, did Kade meet up with you today?"

My heart pounds in my ears as I wait for the response, My mind is already spiraling into worst-case scenarios. There's a scary pause for a few seconds after I ask the question.

He replies casually but with an edge of confusion. "No, man, he didn't show. I thought he got caught or something and ended up going to school instead?"

My breath hitches. "He didn't…? Are you sure? He didn't—?" I can barely get the words out, fear is suffocating me.

"No, nothing. You don't think something's happened to

33

him, do you?" He replies in a concerned tone. I can tell that Aaron isn't lying from the tone of voice and genuine concern.

The question echoes in my head, but it is too late. Panic begins to claw at me as the realisation sinks in. My pulse quickens, the dread sinking deeper with every second. I try to steady my breathing, but all I can think of is what has happened to Kade. What if something went wrong? What if—? My thoughts spin in frantic circles as the world outside seems to be a blur. What if he's been taken…

I start to run down the main street of the town, in quick pursuit of the protest. I'm running quicker than I thought I ever could. The uneven pavement threatens to trip me. My body feels like it's shaking, sweat soaking me profusely. The angry mob storms down the high street toward the police station, but I know a shortcut, one that'll get me there faster. I know I can't get held up in the protest as my point will never be heard by the police. I will simply be one of the many worried public that's screaming at them. If I can reach them before the mob, I can talk to them, one on one, and see if they can look into Kade's disappearance.

I dart left, down a dingy looking alley. It's narrow. The walls are only a few inches either side of me, making me feel as if it's shrinking in on me. The stench of rubbish reeks into my nostrils, causing me to pull a funny face.

Litter and debris cover the ground. Crumpled wrappers and cigarette butts clog parts of the alley aswell, and the stench of stale beer is clinging to the walls. A small black bin is toppled over in front of me. Clearly no one could be bothered to pick it up and everyone was in agreement to just throw their litter wherever they pleased.

I hurdle the bin like a winning racehorse and carry on my sprint, avoiding the array of broken cardboard boxes that spew out from a doorway half way down the passage.

I come out onto a road, filled with masses of stationary cars. Everyone is heading home from work so the backlog of traffic trying to cut through the town is at a standstill.

As I run, I see a glimmer of yellow in the corner of my eye. I can't believe it! It's two police officers who look to be on patrol.

I sprint toward them, pushing my body to its limit. I shout at them. "Hey, Hey officers, I need some help. I fear someone's life might be at stake."

"What seems to be the problem, sir?" says the police officer on the left. He looks like he has spent far too many years in the job to care about anyone else's opinion. His thick, greying eyebrows lift in mockery. I take a look and see his epaulette on the side of his jacket, it reads *'PC Gordon Churchill.'* What an old sounding name. It matched his look to be fair.

"My friend might be in trouble" I say, gasping for air after my run through town.

Rolling his eyes, PC Churchill snaps back. "And what makes you think such a thing is happening?" His reply was sarcastic and unfazed. He has a big bushy moustache that almost muffles his voice as he speaks.

My fists clench after his comment. "Well... there's been loads of disappearances recently."

Before I can finish he interrupts me. "And you think someone you know is gone aswell? I'm sick to death of you people... assuming you've got it all figured out, and that we can do something about it. Maybe they just don't wanna live in this shithole anymore. You lot come running every time someone's late for dinner or doesn't answer their damn phone"

I am completely taken back. Who the hell does he think he is, talking to me like that. I notice the officer to his right looks just as stunned. He clearly hasn't been in the police as long. His uniform is immaculately tidy as if he is trying his best to impress his senior officer. Even his name badge is pristine and in line. PC Marlon Tredon is his name and I can tell just by the way he's standing that he wants to help. He stands tall, a mixture of youthful energy and determination. He looks to be in his mid-twenties. His youthful face seems to be carrying remnants of fresh optimism, which is a big contrast to PC Churchill. His rich brown skin stands out against the cold grey of the city. He has sharp cheekbones and a clean-cut look, like an actor playing a fresh-faced rookie.

Even to PC Churchill's discomfort, PC Tredon chimes in. "So what's happened, can you give me as many details as you can and I'll look into it. Let me make note of it." He swiftly pulls out a small notepad and pen from his right breast pocket and starts writing.

I explain that Kade has bunked off school, going to see his mates, but didn't show up. I explain how I've tried calling him and his friends, but with no luck. I can see him nodding as he is writing, absorbing every little detail. PC Churchill looks a little agitated. Well I guess so would I if I was getting shown up by a much less experienced copper.

"Okay, so I've got all the details. I'm going to start looking into this, I've got your number so will be contacting you with updates as soon as we have some. I would recommend staying safe for now, it seems a dangerous time to be on the streets alone at the moment." His voice is authoritative, yet mixed with concern.

As I'm walking off, I peer back to see PC Churchill scolding his work partner. I don't see why he's got to be such a jerk about it. His slouched posture and the dark rings under his eyes suggest the stress of the job has gotten to him.

SIX
Kade

I start to feel life coming back to my body. A pair of hands grab my shoulders, shaking me awake. Who is this? How long have I been out for? So many questions quickly pass through my head, unsure whether I want to actually find out.

My eyes flicker open, waking up feels like I am surfacing from a deep, murky pool. It takes me a moment to adjust to the lighting, my head feeling even more foggy and heavy than before. I can make out a dark figure above me, still shaking my shoulder, more gently now however. I think whoever it is must realise that I am coming around.

"Hey man, you look a bit worse for wear." says the mysterious man.

As my vision starts to clear, I see him. A tall, broad-shouldered man stands over me, his face looks etched with exhaustion. His skin is deep, rich brown, the kind of hue that absorbs the light rather than reflects it. He has marks all across his face, most notably a big graze on his left cheek that is red with blood. He is wearing a worn, dark grey hoodie and blue denim jeans. The jeans seem to be ripped, not in a fashionable way though, more like the kind that would give off the impression that he'd been dragged through barbed wire. His eyes, dark and tired, meet mine with an intensity that seems to betray the weight of whatever he's been through. There seems

37

to be a quiet desperation in his gaze, a flicker of hope, like what mine probably looked like when I was trying to escape.

"Who are you?" I ask.

He suddenly looks nervous, like he hadn't expected me to wake up and isn't sure what to do now. His voice breaks through the stillness; Low, raspy, like he's been talking to no one for too long. "Name's Carl. Damn, you're alive... Thought I was the only one left. Where are we? What the fuck is this place? We have to get out!"

"How did you move from your bed? Everyone seemed to be tied down." I ask. I didn't see him earlier, however there were still around four or five beds that I was left to check. Some of them had blankets that covered what I assumed were bodies, so it's very plausible that I missed him.

"I woke up about ten minutes ago. I have no idea where we are, but I saw this crazy man in a lab coat injecting something in your arm. I didn't know if you were alive or not. I kept quiet and pretended to be out until he left, I was over there in the corner. I couldn't even tell you how long I've been here for, what day is it?" He points to the far side of the room as he is talking. It was where I didn't get a chance to look last time. Carl also adds "I don't know when he will be back so I think we should make a move."

I don't know this man. I shouldn't trust him, but something in his eyes... it's real. His fear, his desperation, it's the same I've felt. I need to trust someone, don't I?

He also just said the doctor injected something into my arm... He's already been experimenting on me, but what kind of sick experiments? The Brute... What if I end up like him? Like a mindless monster? What if it's already happening? Maybe this isn't even real, maybe it's some sort of sick nightmare. No, this can't be real. It doesn't feel real. My head is spinning, my body feels wrong, like it's not even mine anymore. What the hell did he inject into me? My fingers twitch involuntarily. What if it's already working? What if I turn into—No. No, I can't think like that. I have to stay in control. But what if it's too late?

I go to sit up, but spot that I have now been fully tied to the bed. Not by chains though, I threw the padlock and chain to the side when I got up last time and the doctor probably couldn't find them. I've got a few leather belts and some rope tightly fastened around my wrists and ankles, strapping me close to the bed. They are fastened on tightly, I can feel my wrists pulsating against the belts.

"See if you can find anything sharp to cut me free." I ask. I can see Carl searching the room. The tools that were previously on the floor have been moved and the shards of glass have been swept up. The Doc must have learned from last time and made it harder for me to free myself.

Carl scrambles through the corner, his movements frantic. He's back in seconds, gripping a jagged piece of metal like it's a lifeline. It looks like something that has broken off one of the metal tables perhaps. He puts it to the rope and belts that bound me to this table and manages to use it to hacksaw me free.

It feels like such a relief. I examine my wrists, the straps have left red markings around them.

Carl takes a few steps towards the door and examines it. Even though he is crouched, Carl's massive build blocks most of the view of the door. The quiet crunch of glass beneath his feet stands out in the otherwise silent room.

"It's an old metal door, like the ones they use in those big freezer rooms. I don't think we can barge this down." mutters Carl.

"The Doc had keys, but I bet he took them, maybe we can look for another way out?" I respond.

I examine the room, beginning my search for anything that can help us escape. The walls around me are cold, the kind of sterile, industrial surface that seems to hum with a quiet, oppressive energy. My breath feels shallow as I move around the room, each inhale is thin and sharp in the heavy air. As I pace the room, my eyes are scanning for anything that might give me a way out. The faint hum of the lights echo through the space, a constant reminder that we're being watched, studied, trapped.

I walk to the far side of the lab, trying to avoid making any noise. Metal tables are littered with half-finished projects, strange, unidentifiable tools, and pieces of equipment that look more like science fiction than anything you'd expect to find in a real lab. But none of it seems useful. None of it is a way out. There's nothing here. The doors are locked, reinforced beyond reason. The vents are too small to crawl through, and the walls are too thick to break. I'm trapped.

In the far corner of the room I can see a stack of old cardboard boxes, pushed haphazardly against one of the walls. It looks out of place, even for this lab. My curiosity spikes, and I approach it cautiously, the sound of my footsteps is soft against the dirty, tiled floor. The cardboard is battered, creased from age, and there's something strange about how it's stacked. It's almost as if it's been moved recently, trying to block something maybe.

I pull one of the boxes away from the wall. It's a lot heavier than I expected it to be. It's probably filled with a load more junk. Probably tools that the crazy bastard was going to use to test on us. I manage to shift it to the side. My heartbeat spikes as I realise what I've uncovered. It's a window, hidden behind the cardboard. It feels as though it is glowing. This is it. This is our way out.

I signal to Carl to come over. He was busy searching

some of the tables for tools to try and pry the door open with. When he sees the window his face lights up. He moves quickly to me, almost skipping and jumping with joy and excitement.

The small window appears to be boarded up with some wood. It looks like some sort of bodged job at covering it. Most of the light has been blocked but it appears to only have a few nails to hold it in place.

Carl pushes me aside, grabbing onto one of the planks of wood. He pulls with ease and pries the wood away. He looks at the wood in his hand with surprise, as if he never expected it to come off that easily. "This isn't normal" he murmurs, his hands shaking with shock.

I can't help but think, how did he do that? Most men would struggle to even pry it away slightly, and he has just taken the whole thing off with ease. He tries again with the same lack of difficulty when pulling the other board. Maybe he has got some sort of super strength. Maybe the doctor has been testing on him before he woke up.

Behind the boards we can see that there is a musty glass window, covered in dust and dirt. It looks like it hasn't been cleaned in years. Carl uses his sleeve to wipe away some of the dirt so that we can peer out.

The other side of the window looks dark. It must be nearly night time. It appears that the room we are in is below ground level. The window is high up on the inside, so we would have to climb to get out of it. But it seems to be quite low to the ground on the other side.

"Should we just smash it?" queries Carl.

"If we do, we're going to have to get out quickly, there's no way the doctor doesn't hear that." I respond. I take a look behind us to see if there's anything we can use to force our way through the window and escape through the opening. As I'm scouring the nearby surfaces, a bright white flash lights up the room…

SMASH!!!

I immediately crouch slightly, putting my hands over my head for cover. What the hell was that? Is the doctor back?

I look back to Carl to see the glass is smashed to pieces. It is scattered along the floor and around the frame of the window. Carl appears to be holding his hand in disbelief again. He looks like he has seen a ghost.

"What the hell was that?" I ask in a quiet yet authoritative tone. He's not only strong. He must have some sort of super punch. One that gives off some bright flash when he connects with his target.

"I don't know how I did that… It just… happened" murmurs Carl. He looks shook.

THUD … *THUD* … "THUD" …

The sound of footsteps coming from the other side of the metal door echoes throughout the room. Carl panics and tries to hoist his large, heavy frame up towards the windows. Even though there's all the smashed glass around the frame it doesn't faze him, as he knows this might be his only chance of escape. I run and lift his legs as he pulls himself up. His body and the gap of the windows are almost the same size, squeezing his frame through is almost impossible. I try with all my might to push Carl through the gap.

Carl manages to get through to the other side and stands up. He stops for a second. I can see him looking around taking in the surroundings. The chill air coasts through the window, breezing into the room.

"By the look of it, the lab is in an old and abandoned wooden house. It's in the middle of a dense overgrown Forest." Carl says as he extends his arm down to grab me.

My muscles scream in protest as I scramble up, my hands slipping on the jagged frame. The footsteps are nearly at the door now; too close. Too fast.

As I'm trying to fit through, I can see green ferns that surround us. They do a great job of hiding the window from anyone that would walk past. There are fallen logs and trees everywhere as if the area of nature hadn't been tampered with once. There are leaves covering the floor like a carpet, which do a good job of covering the uneven terrain. The air smells rich with earth and pine, the scent of moss and damp leaves hanging heavily in the cool breeze.

I turn as my body gets pulled out. I look up to see the house for myself. It's an old wooden cabin, weathered and half-hidden by the encroaching underbrush. The cabin looks like it has stood here for decades, maybe even centuries. Its timbers are darkened by age and neglect, its roof looks like it could be sagging under the weight of years of moss and fallen leaves. The rest of the windows are clouded with dirt and grime, seeming to stare out like hollow eyes, blank and uninviting.

I am just about to stand when something sharp hits me in my back. I turn and pull out some sort of tranquilizer dart. It's got a fluffy yellow end to it, looking like something you'd see a ranger use to tranquilize a lion on a safari. I show it to Carl as my body starts to fall, just in front of the window. My vision is starting to blur and my hands are feeling tingly, as if I've got really bad pins and needles.

The doctor is in the lab, walking towards the window with a scary demeanor. I look up at Carl, helpless as my body's going numb. The lights flicker slightly, casting a flashing shadow, as the labcoated maniac edges ever closer.

I try to make a sound to Carl, my lips going numb. I have to see if I can get him to pick me up, but the sound coming out of my mouth is unrecognisable, almost sounding like some sort of pathetic whimper. Carl looks past me, towards the doctor.

He dives out of the way of something. A dart whizzes past, thudding into a nearby tree. I can see Carl look up for a second, debating whether saving me is worth the risk.

He mouths the words "I'm sorry"

"Carl… wait! Don't leave me here!" My voice slurs, barely audible. He stops. Just for a second. His fists clench. Then he's gone.

As he runs, he doesn't take a second look back for me. I feel utterly betrayed. He has left me like an injured carcass, feeding me to the lions. I mean, could I fully blame him? What could he do? My body goes still, and despite my best effort, I fall asleep again…

SEVEN
Marlon

PC Churchill and PC Tredon,
Following the case of Kade Astons disappearance, I
want you two to go to the last known area that he was found.
We know that he got the A231, the bus that took him out of the
city, and got off at around 08:03. After this he was last seen
starting his journey North on Whistler's Hollow Road. At 08:31
a witness drove through that road, however, did not see Kade
or any other people. See what you can find, and bring back any
evidence that you can.
Thanks, Sargent Wendy Davis.
- ***Text message from Sargent Wendy Davis to PC***
Gordon Churchill — Sunday, 13th April 2025

PC Churchill and I are driving through town. We're on
our way down to where Kade was reportedly last dropped off
by the bus the morning he disappeared.

As we move through the streets we can see that the
once beautiful town, filled with a rich history and fascinating
agriculture is now crumbling, a shadow of what it once was.
Graffiti scars the walls, the only splash of color in a town
drained of life. The buildings look grey and lifeless, with
cracks snaking up and down the walls.

The last remnants of nature in the city are dying,

overgrown beyond recognition. Small grass patches near the walkways of the street are spewing out weeds, some making their way onto the paths. It's a sorry sight. It feels like a forgotten corner of the country, abandoned to fend for itself and rot.

There is even a stench of rotting waste that is somehow seeping through the nearly closed windows of the police car. I don't know where it's coming from, and I don't want to. I wind the window up to fully close and block out the smell.

Krrrrr The police radio crackles to life. "All units near Southside, multiple animal carcasses reported at Black Water Farm. Details unknown. Any available units, respond. Over."

"This is DC Emily Langford, I'm only half a mile away so heading there now, over."

Dead animal carcasses? That's not something you hear every day. What the hell could've done that? I run my hands through my short, curly black hair as I try to think. My thoughts are quickly interrupted.

"Look at her, why's she moving like that?" barks Churchill while pointing in front of the car.

I can't tell where he's pointing. He must have caught something I missed, a flicker of movement, something out of place.

"Where are you pointing? I can't tell." I ask.

Churchill quickly snaps again "Look" and nods towards the corner of a butcher's shop around twenty meters ahead of us.

Just barely visible, a woman is crouched behind the edge of the building. Her head seems to be peeking around the corner with a slight tilt. Her red headband, bright and noticeable, holds back her dark hair, standing out against the grey concrete of the building. She seems to be watching the street with intense focus, her eyes darting between the passing cars as if waiting for something, or someone.

Churchill squints, narrowing his gaze. "She's not blending in," he mutters, his hand drifts towards the radio that's clipped to his belt.

"Why hide if she's not doing anything wrong?" I ask.

Churchill pauses, studying her movements. "There is something cautious, almost rehearsed, about the way she's shifting. She barely peeks her head around the corner, hiding most of her body."

Before I can get a clearer look, she slips back into the shadows, vanishing like she was never there at all.

"Something about her stance felt off, like she didn't want to be noticed... but didn't realise she already was." I say with a confused tone.

"I was about to call it in, but... she's gone. We'll have to keep an eye out on the way back." replies Churchill.

We start to move out of the town, towards the more desolate area, where the absence of human life is palpable. It's hard to think that only a few hundred meters away from all the buildings is the complete polar opposite. Not that you would want to be there, but it's spewing with people, usually far too many.

We arrive at Whistler's Hollow Road, the road that the bus stop is on. As we roll through, I think it's a really bizarre place for a bus stop to be, there's not much here at all. You'd expect there to at least be a small cafe or a fuel station or something on this road, but there's literally nothing. The only thing I can see is a few winding footpaths coming off the main road into the overgrown wooded area. It's not that big of a wooded area, probably a few hundred trees that stretch back around thirty meters or so.

We park up at a small layby on the side of the road

near the bus stop and get out of the car.

"So... the bus stop is here, apparently that skatepark place is up the road north. I'm assuming he started walking to it on foot, so let's do the same. See if we can find anything abnormal." says Churchill.

I'll be honest, Churchill wasn't exactly my first choice of partners. When I was told a few weeks ago that I would be paired up with him for a while, I wasn't best pleased. He's always been so old and grumpy, like he's always got some sort of chip on his shoulder. His short temper seems to snap, anytime something out of the normal happens. He's very old school in the way he deals with people though, and doesn't take shit off anyone. I've heard stories from some of my co-workers that when he worked on nights, he would constantly be seen yelling at the younger drunk males that were wandering the street misbehaving. They all used to listen to him and I don't blame them.

We walk for a few minutes and I hear Churchill shout from in front of me. "Hey, look over here!" His voice sounds so much more focused on the task than when he first heard about it.

I knew he didn't believe the stories about people going missing, but now that we're here his attitude has changed. I guess he realises that it is a genuine case and not one of those concerning partner jobs. You know, the ones where they're not actually missing, they just didn't pick up their phone. We get them a lot.

I can see him pointing to the ground, so I carry on walking towards him and look down. There are a few tyre skid marks on the ground that spread along for around ten meters or so. I can see Churchill tracing over some of them with his finger, trying to imagine what went down. The streaks suggest that whoever was here was going fast and had to stop in a hurry.

I kneel down to the ground to take a closer look. I can see a few remnants of smashed glass, glittered along the tarmac like cruel stars, reflecting the sun's beams directly into our eyes.

I turn and look at Churchill again, his eyes fixated on a dark smear of blood that's marred the gravel shoulder. It isn't a large pool, but its presence speaks volumes. Churchill turns to look at me and we both stare at each other with a concerned glance. Neither of us seem to want to exchange words, however I know exactly what he is thinking.

I finally muster up the courage to say something. "That's weird… someone definitely got hit here. Whether it's Kade or not, something happened here recently, and I want to find out what."

"The problem is, this place is in the middle of bloody nowhere. You could scream and no one would hear a sound. It's no wonder that no one saw anything, and no one even knows what happened," says Churchill.

I see Churchill take out his phone and begin to take some pictures of the scene. He then pulls out a tape measure. I can see him measuring the length of the tracks and gaps between the skid marks. I take out a swab and collect a small sample of the blood that's stained on the side of the road.

"Have a walk up and down the road. See if you can see any footprints." Suggests Churichill in a commanding voice.

I get up from the bloodstain and start to pace up and down the road. I'm looking for any sort of sign that someone left the scene. Whether it be footprints, more blood or even broken shrubbery that looks like it could have been caused by a human passing through, I want to find it.

I've now searched for around twenty minutes but can't seem to find anything. No signs of anyone coming off the road or anything.

I can hear the faint hum of an engine coming over the hill. Something peeks over and I can see that it's another police car that's approaching us. They're here to tape off the area so that no more cars can come in and contaminate the crime scene.

Me and Churchill walk back to the car before getting in it. We have to take the collected samples with us for forensic examination, aswell as the notes we've made to try and figure out what vehicle it was. Churchill starts the engine up and we begin our journey back to the station.

EIGHT
Duncan

It's been A few days since I last spoke to PC Churchill and PC Tredon. Even though it's late in the day, I'm still anxiously waiting for a call from them about Kade. This feels like a suffocating mix of hope and dread, where every second seems to stretch out, unbearably long.

I sit by my phone, unable to focus on anything else. I try to put the TV on, but I can't concentrate. My eyes keep flicking to my phone screen every few minutes to check if I've somehow missed it ringing. I know I've got it on loud speaker, but I just can't help but look. The silence in the room feels oppressive, it's heavy with unanswered questions. Each small sound I hear, whether it be a creak in the floorboards, or the distant hum of a passing car makes my heart jump, as if it could be the signal of some news. I know it's silly but my senses are in hyperdrive.

My mind starts to race through every possibility; the good, the terrifying, and everything in between. I'm simply cycling through desperate prayers and dark imaginings that I can't seem to stop. I feel my stomach twist with nausea, my chest tighten with anxiety. Even breathing is feeling like a chore as I sit still, gripping the edge of my chair, as if holding onto something solid will keep me grounded.

I think of my best friend; His smile, his laugh, his

51

confidence. I know that he'd know exactly what to do in this situation. He wouldn't just be sitting here waiting for a phone call. Kade is the kind of guy that would be out searching all night and all day, and here I am, cowardly waiting for a phone call from the police.

I log onto my laptop and decide to print off some posters to stick around town. Maybe if I add my number to the bottom of it aswell, they might ring me if they know something.

Just as I finish making the poster, the thought of where he might be crashes over me again. Time has been moving in strange loops these past few days, minutes feeling like hours, hours feeling like days.

Brrring... Brrring... Brrring... My phone finally starts to ring. I feel my breath start to catch in my throat, fear and hope are colliding as I reach out with trembling hands. I'm unsure whether the voice on the other end will bring relief or shatter me further, but I have to find out.

"Hello?" I answer tentatively.

"Hello, is this Duncan? PC Churchill calling." The voice says.

"Yes it is… Are there any updates? Have you found him?" I reply with far too much hesitation, but I can't seem to stop myself from stuttering.

"So, We haven't found him yet, but we are chasing some very creditable leads. We're going to need you to come into the station if possible please. We need to do another interview as we've got some extra questions that we need answers to. If possible, are you able to pop down sometime today please." His voice sounds a lot more serious when talking to him this time, rather than before when he was being a jerk.

"Yeah, sure thing, I'll get my Mum to drop me off and

head there right away." I reply.

I can't help but worry about what sort of questions they're going to ask. Do they think I did something to him? Are they going to give me some bad news? My mind starts to race again.

I quickly head down the stairs and into the living room where my Mum is sitting down on the sofa.

Nervously I ask "Hi Mum… is there any chance you can give me a lift to the police station…" my eyes start to swell slightly. I can't help but let out a few tears as I finish my sentence. I'm so scared, I just want Kade back. My Mum sees me shedding a few tears and immediately gets off the sofa, rushing to comfort me, burying me in her arms.

"What's wrong sweety?" Her voice is soothing, with a concerned yet calming tone.

"I'm just struggling. I can't help but think that this is all my fault. I should have told him to come back to school and not kept covering for him. I knew it wasn't right and I'm so sorry." I needed to get this off my chest. It's been burning me for days, I can't keep it in. Knowing that if I didn't let him bunk off school he'd still be here with us. Instead he's out there somewhere, god knows what's happened.

I add "I've printed off a load of posters with Kade's face on it saying missing, and put my number on it to contact. I'm thinking of posting them around the street after I've been to the station, I don't know what else to do. What do you think the police want? Will they be angry at me for lying for him so he could bunk off?"

"No, of course they won't be mad at you," she says while giving me another hug and rubbing the back of my head. "And for the posters, I think it's a great idea, I've already been posting it everywhere online. Fifty people have already reposted it. The more people that we can get looking the better, he's going to show up somewhere, I know it."

After an emotional few minutes I pack my bag with all the freshly printed posters and a staple gun. I'm not sure if it's the type of thing that I should take to a police station but I don't care. Me and my Mum head out the front door and get in the car, ready to get to the station.

NINE
Duncan

I can't help but feel like I'm being followed everywhere I go. I left London to get away from them, but maybe they've followed me here. I'm also hearing voices everywhere I go, I think I'm going crazy.

- ***Unknown Journal entry — Monday, 14th April 2025***

"Thanks Mum, love you" I say as my Mum puts the car into gear. I can't help but look back at her, wanting her to come in with me. Her sweet smile lifts as I say the words.

"Love you too, let me know how it goes" she replies as she winds up the window and pulls away to drive down the road.

I turn around and look up, hesitant as I stand there at the front steps of the police station. My trainers are scuffing against the concrete as I stand there trying to calm my jittery hands. The building looms before me, looking old and weathered, its bricks are streaked with years of grime. There's a flickering fluorescent bulb buzzing faintly above the entrance, lighting up the police station sign; also casting a pale, sickly light onto the ground. The large glass doors in front of me bores smudges, likely from countless grimey hands pushing the door open. I catch a quick distorted glimpse of my pale, anxious face in the door, it reflects back at me, staring me

55

down.

I push open the left door nervously, slowly entering my body into the station. Inside, the station is surprisingly cold and unwelcoming, the walls are painted a dull beige that seems to amplify my unease. The air smells faintly of stale coffee and industrial cleaning supplies. It's no surprise with the coffee smell. I bet with all the stress of the job a lot of caffeine would be needed to get through the day.

There's a scuffed linoleum floor stretched before me, its tiles are arranged in a drab checkerboard pattern that seems to mirror the mood of the place. I think the place could do with a makeover or a few flowers or something, just to brighten the place up. I know it shouldn't be the most glamorous of places but this is taking the mick.

I walk forward to the reception desk that's sat directly ahead of me, manned by a middle-aged officer whose weary expression suggests that he had seen far too much for one lifetime. Just by the look of this guy, he sort of reminds me of PC Churchill. I hope all the officers aren't as grumpy as him.

Behind the officer, rows of filing cabinets loom, like sentinels guarding years of forgotten cases. Some of them are not even shut properly, papers are crammed inside and spew out of the top. The walls are cluttered with bulletin boards, each one plastered with curling papers: crime alerts, safety notices, and mugshots pinned with careless thumbtacks. A large clock ticks ominously above the reception area, each second a sharp reminder of how time drags in places like these. There is a corridor behind the desk to the right, I wonder where it leads.

I swallow hard and force myself to meet the officer's gaze. "I—I'm here about... my friend. The missing one," I stammer, my voice barely above a whisper.

The officer gives me a quick nod, motioning for me to

wait on a cracked vinyl bench along the wall. I walk over and sit down, my leg bouncing nervously, the plastic squeaking beneath me.

I sit there for a few moments, staring at the cracked floor and bouncing my leg. I feel like the clock above the reception is ticking just for me, dragging time along as I wait.

Then, out of the corner of my eye, I see a woman in a police uniform walking down the hallway, her purposeful steps cutting through the space like she's in a rush. She passes by without looking at me at first, but then her eyes catch mine, and she slows, giving me a curious but friendly glance.

"Hey, you okay?" she asks, her voice warm, though there's a hint of something else underneath. Her eyes flicker over me, studying me but not in an intrusive way. "You look like you've got something heavy on your mind."

I feel a little caught off guard at first, unsure what to say. It's only then that I notice her name badge, *'DC Emily Langford'*, and her kind expression softens a bit of the tension in my chest.

"I… uh, yeah, I'm alright. I just—my mate, he's been missing for a few days now," I say, shifting in my seat, the words tasting foreign in my mouth.

Langford's expression softens immediately. She steps closer, her voice lowering slightly, more personal. "I'm really sorry to hear that," she says, nodding as though she can understand. "I know it must be tough, especially with everything going on in the world."

She pauses for a second, glancing at the reception desk like she's making sure no one's watching before taking a seat next to me on the bench. Her eyes are kind, but there's a depth to them that makes me feel like she's seen this kind of thing before.

"You're not alone in this, alright?" she says softly, her

words thoughtful. "I know it might not feel like it, but you've got people here who care. Missing persons cases, they can drag on, but that doesn't mean we stop looking. Not by a long shot."

I nod, feeling a lump form in my throat, but I'm trying not to show it. I didn't expect anyone to actually get it, not like this, not like her.

"I just… I don't know where to even start, you know?" I say, rubbing the back of my neck. "Feels like there's no answers, and I'm just waiting around in the dark."

Langford gives me a sympathetic smile, a hint of determination in her eyes. "Sometimes that's all we can do," she says. "But you're doing the right thing by coming to the station, asking and answering questions. You've got to start somewhere." She gives me a reassuring look, almost like she's been in my shoes before.

"Thanks," I mumble, still feeling uneasy. I wasn't expecting comfort, but she gave it without hesitation, like it was second nature to her.

She stands up, adjusting her belt as she gets ready to leave. "I'm sure we'll find something soon. Just don't forget to lean on the people around you. This kind of thing, it's tough on your own."

I watch her walk toward the hallway, my heart heavy, but lighter than it was when she first approached.

"Thanks, DC Langford," I call after her, my voice steadier now.

She glances over her shoulder, a small smile tugging at her lips. "Anytime. Just hang in there, alright?"

She disappears down the hall, and I sit there for a moment, feeling a little less alone.

About thirty seconds later, two figures emerge from the corridor behind the receptionist. It's PC Churchill and PC Tredon.

PC Churchill puts out his hand and says "Thanks for coming on such short notice Duncan. Can you follow us to one of the interview rooms please? This shouldn't take long."

I shake his hand while saying "Okay, no problem, let me know what you need me to answer and I'll do my best." I can't help but feel the way that he worded it, sounds like I might be in trouble.

PC Churchill looks slightly less grumpy than he did a few days ago, while PC Tredon looks even more focused. His freshly shaved face is unreadable, as if every expression's tucked away behind duty and habit. His light skin catches the light from one of the hanging fluorescent lights, but it does nothing to soften the focused look in his eyes.

I get up to follow them and as I walk down the corridor, my gaze darts around the room. Through an open doorway to the left, I can see a bullpen filled with desks, each piled high with papers, cluttered with empty coffee cups and scattered pens. To the right, I see a series of heavy metal doors, each marked with a faded stenciled number.

Are they leading to the interrogation room I wonder? Maybe one of these cell doors might soon open for me.

We walk to the end of the corridor, the ten meters we've travelled feels like forever. I can see this is some sort of interrogation or interview room. It looks just like the movies. A big darked out mirror (definitely a one way mirror) extends to nearly the whole wall. This makes me nervous, what if they think it's me.

"Take a seat Duncan" asks PC Tredon.

PC Churchill says "Okay, so everything said here is going to be recorded, just for our records... so, where to begin." Scratching his head he adds "Thanks for coming in to talk to us. Just to confirm, you're here voluntarily, yeah?"

I reply, "Yep, of course. I want to help. Kade's a good

mate of mine, and I'm worried about him."

"Good to hear. Before we start, we need to go through the formalities. For the record, you're not under arrest or anything, and you're free to leave at any time. If there's anything you're not comfortable answering, just let us know. These are just some following questions that we want confirming after your witness statement." PC Tredon adds

"Understood." I reply

PC Churchill probes "Right, so we're trying to piece together a timeline of events leading up to Kade's disappearance three days ago. When did you last see him exactly?"

The pressure from their voices and the spotlight beaming down on me makes me feel uneasy, I'm losing my train of thought and it's only the first question. "That'd be... last Friday morning, we left as he went to get on the bus to meet his friends, I got on the bus to go to school." I stutter.

PC Tredon nods his head and queries "When you left him, did you notice anyone else nearby?"

"When I left him, I'll be honest, I didn't really notice anyone, but that's not to say they weren't there, I just wasn't exactly looking out for anyone." I try to think of anyone who was there, but I can't really remember. There were bound to be loads of people passing by at that time.

"Has Kade seemed different lately? Any signs he was stressed or worried about anything?"

"No, not at all. He's been his usual self; cracking jokes, being the life of the party as usual." I say.

He quickly snaps back saying "And no arguments or falling-outs with anyone?"

"No, god no. Nothing like that. Everyone gets on with Kade. He's a good kid." I can't help but feel that question was aimed at me.

PC Churchill also asks "Right, since Friday, have you tried getting in touch with him?"

I know I've tried, but he hasn't picked up, so I have to tell them that. "Yeah, I've called and texted loads, but his phone's off. I even tried to call his friends that he was supposed to meet, but there was no sign of him."

PC Tredon poses "Do you know if he's got anywhere else he might go? Family, other mates? Stuff like that."

I reply "His family aren't around now, they died in a car crash around three months ago. He started living with me and my Mum not long after that. As for mates, I think I know most of them. None of them have seen him either."

PC Churchill finally asks "Alright, Duncan, thanks for answering everything so far. Is there anything else you can think of that might help us find Kade?"

I can't really think of anything else to add, so nervously I say "I don't think so. I mean, he'd usually let someone know if he was going away or something. This just isn't like him at all."

PC Tredon mutters "Understood. If you do think of anything, no matter how small it seems, give us a ring, alright?" He is definitely a lot more friendly in his tone compared to PC Churchill.

I reply, "Yeah, of course."

I'm curious to see what they know, they've been so busy trying to find out what information I have, but if I'm going to help find him, I want to know something. A lead maybe, something I can chase up on.

"So… what are the leads that you've got? I'm trying to help find him aswell, I would like to know if possible." I press, leaning forward as I do so.

"Well… it's not so easy for us to just tell you all that we know. Some of it is confidential information." I can see that

61

me asking the question has made the pair slightly uneasy. PC Tredon appears to be brushing a bit of sweat off his forehead, whilst PC Churchill is staying still.

"Well... what can you tell me? The non-confidential bits that is." I swing back.

PC Tredon chimes in and says "So... we know that when you and Kade split in the morning, he got the A231 bus and got off at Whistler's Hollow Road. Now from there is where we can't piece together. We don't believe that he is anywhere near there now, so if you could, don't head there as it is still an investigation site. There were some signs of an incident there."

"What do you mean by incident?" I snap back quickly. What could that mean? Was he taken? Is he dead?

Officer Tredon looks shocked, small amounts of sweat glisten off his short, curly black hair. PC Churchill starts casting a deathly glance over to him, he looks disappointed. I don't think he was supposed to give me that bit of information.

"Now... um... when I say incident, I don't mean anything bad has happened... we just don't know what he did from there."

PC Churchill backs him up saying "We have been speaking to different witnesses, trying to map out what happened. It's only a matter of time before this gets resolved." The way that he spoke that almost made it seem like a cover up. Almost as if there was more information that they are not telling me.

As they're talking some more I can't help but glance down to the paperwork on the desk. I can see that there is a file that says *'Kade Aston'* at the top in big handwritten letters. It looks like some sort of printed out email or something. I can't make out all the text as it's partially hidden under a folder.

More work is laid out on the desk. One of the papers

seems to be focused on some unknown attacks. I can see part of the picture and it looks like something out of a horror film. There's blood, gore, guts, all coming out of some sort of animal. I'm no forensic expert but I can tell that whatever did that isn't human.

"Anyway, I think that's all the information we needed, thankyou" says PC Tredon, cutting me from my search across the desk. They both get up to try and signal the end of the questioning so I do the same and get up.

The pair of them walk past me and go to the door to open it. In a panicked rush of blood I grab the paper document that has Kade's name scribbled on it and hide it in my hoodie, trying my best to not let it stick out. Luckily the hoodie I'm wearing is quite baggy so I can hide it easily.

We make the slow walk back to the front of the station together. This feels even more stressful than the journey in. The first time I thought I was in trouble, now this time I know I'll get in trouble if they catch me.

I can see both officers side eyeing me slightly, almost weighing me up. I'm not sure if my nerves are giving me away. I have got a hand in the hoodie pocket, stopping the paper from falling out. With every step I pray that the paper doesn't make a loud rustle to give me away.

TEN
Duncan

The station door creaks behind me as I step out into the cold night air. My breath fogs up instantly, swirling like a ghost in front of me. It feels nice to be on this side of the door again; lighter almost, though my chest is still tight, not allowing me to exhale fully. I tug my hoodie tighter around me, the rough fabric brushing against the stack of posters stuffed in my bag. My hand is still desperately clenched to the document about Kade, I can't let go until I am far enough away.

I reach into my bag and run my fingers over the corners of the posters, their edges curling slightly from the rush of shoving them in earlier. *'Missing'* they all say in bold letters, along with his face. Kade's face. It's a good picture. One of him, from when we went on holiday together last year, before he got mixed up in whatever this is. I printed twenty of them. Twenty chances for someone to see him, to say something.

I take my hand out of the bag and into my hoodie pocket again. My fingers brushing into the path of the small crumpled up piece of paper, and I freeze. I shouldn't have taken it. I know that. But the way it was just left there, so casually, as if it wasn't the most important thing in the world... it was too easy not to take. I quickly bury it to the bottom of my bag. I glance back to make sure no one was looking. I think I'm all clear and no one saw, well not yet, anyway. I shove my hands

64

into my pockets and start walking.

The posters rustle with every step I take, a quiet reminder of what's at stake. I know I need to get these up tonight, even if it means wandering through every dark corner of this town. Kade's out there somewhere. I don't know if he's scared or hurt or... worse. I owe it to him to keep looking.

Just up ahead I see a wooden telephone pole, lit up by a nearby lamppost, almost being highlighted. This is where I start. I reach back into my bag, grab the first poster aswell as the staple gun and attach it to the wall.

I go around for around thirty minutes, stapling posters wherever I can. The more public the place, the better. I have the last one in hand as I approach Ravenwood Square. I can see that Tony's Pizzas is still open. This is usually a hot spot for the people of the town on an evening like this. They're the best pizzas in town. There is a free car park just around the back so it is ideal for ordering and picking up for a quick, cheat meal.

I walk inside the pizza shop, Antonio working hard as usual. He hears me come in and lifts his head up. "Hey my man, how's it going, I haven't seen you or your mate come in here for a while now, good to see you back."

He wipes his hands on a tea towel and walks over, the overhead lights catching the silver strands in his greying hair. Antonio's in his late fifties, with olive-toned skin, wiry but still active, always moving like he's got a dozen things to do. He's got that kind of quiet Italian charm about him, though the creases around his eyes look deeper than they used to.

I can't help but feel downed by his comment, another reminded of my current solitude without my best mate. "Yeah... he's not around at the moment... He went missing a few days ago" I stammer.

I can see he looks visibly upset at the comment. "I'm so sorry to hear that. I know how you're feeling. My wife,

65

Sophia, she's missing too" he whispers.

"Is it okay if I leave a poster here... I feel the more people that know the faces of who're missing, the better. Maybe someone might have some insight." I ask cautiously. I know it's a sore subject at the moment and I don't want to push it but I feel this would be a great place for people to have eyes on the poster.

"Go ahead, I've already got one of my Sophia up, put it next to that..." He pauses as if he cuts off what he was going to say.

"Everything okay?" I question.

"Yes... It's just you see. I've had some contact with someone. Someone that might know something. She said not to tell anyone, but you're in just as much of a ruck as me." I can tell by his voice he wants to keep her word but I need to know.

"Who is she, and what does she know?" I press.

"Well... I don't know her name... She came in yesterday after closing. She said she thinks Sophia has gotten involved in something bad. She wouldn't go into details, but by the sounds of it she was having some sort of breakdown. As if she was talking to herself at times, arguing with voices inside her head maybe... Anyway, she got spooked and got off. I tried to shout for her, but she'd gone by the time I got out the front."

What the hell sort of thing is this? How would that mystery woman, Kade and Sophia be connected? I need to try to do some more digging.

I tell him "Thanks for letting me in on it, seems to me like she was a bit of a nut job. Maybe it's true, maybe it's not. I'm going to keep sniffing around until I find something. I'll let you know as soon as I hear anything."

As I walk out of the pizza shop I look into the now poster-free bag, the only thing left is the document. I'm going to open that tonight and look through it properly, maybe it'll contain a clue. I should get home before it's too dark.

I bring out my phone, my hands shivering as I do so, and ring my Mum to come pick me up.

ELEVEN
Duncan

The second I step into my room, I shut the door, leaning against it to not let anyone in. I'm breathing hard, harder than usual anyway. My room smells faintly of stale laundry and the lingering scent of Mum's fabric softener. It was familiar, safe, but tonight, it felt different. It's like I was bringing something dangerous into a space that wasn't ready for it. The whole car journey home I was thinking, this is all some kind of conspiracy, it has to be. It can't be a coincidence that all these people are going missing, and this mystery woman that spoke to Antonio was saying they're involved in something dangerous. I have to find out what's going on.

Maybe this woman is the key to this. Finding her is going to be a problem though. By the sound of it, she's paranoid, almost as if she felt she had to watch what she said.

I open my bag, unzipping it quickly, sending my hand diving down to the bottom. The paper has crumpled quite a bit, but it is still readable. My fingers are still shaking. I hadn't planned on stealing it, well, not really. When I saw it lying there in the interrogation room, half-buried under a stack of papers, I knew I couldn't just walk away. Not without answers. Not without something to explain where Kade has gone.

I look at the paper, Kade's name in big letters at the top is staring me in the face. This has to be it, this has to be a clue

68

as to where he is.

A knock at the door snaps me out of it. "Duncan?" Mum's voice, soft but worried. "You sure you don't want a drink or some food? You've hardly eaten today."

I quickly run to my bed and shove the paper under my pillow, my heart lurching. "I'm okay thanks, I… ate something earlier." That was a total lie, I hadn't eaten all day, and the way that came out of my mouth didn't sound anywhere near as convincing as I thought it would.

There was a pause. I could picture her standing there, hand resting on the doorframe, frowning the way she always did when she didn't quite believe me. "You okay? You sound… off."

"I'm fine, Mum. Really. Just tired."

Another pause. Longer this time. Then: "Alright. But if you need to talk about anything—"

"I'm good. Thanks."

She hesitates again before her footsteps retreat down the hall. I wait until I can't hear her anymore, then I grab the paper, sliding it out from under my pillow.

I feel awful cutting her off, I just don't know what to do. Do I tell her that I think something bad is going on? Do I not? She worries enough as it is, I don't want to put her in that position. Especially if this ends up being something over nothing.

I walk back to the door, reclaiming my seated position with my back to the door.

I look at the paper, it reads:

'Subject: *Update on Investigation: Missing Person –* Kade Aston

Dear PC Gordon Churchill,

I hope this email finds you well. I am writing to provide an update on the ongoing investigation into the disappearance

69

of Kade Aston, Case ID: #48625

As discussed in our previous briefing, the following points have been addressed:

- **Witness Interviews:** *Two additional witnesses have come forward, providing further information on Kade's last known movements. Notes from these interviews are attached for your review.*

- **Surveillance Footage:** *One piece of CCTV footage from the A231 bus has been retrieved and is currently being analyzed. Preliminary observations suggest a possible lead, which I will discuss further in our next meeting.*

- **Evidence Review:** *Forensic analysis on the items recovered from Whistler's Hollow Road is completed and previously submitted. However, Forensics on the items recovered from the Black Water Farm incident is completed and some seem to match those at Whitler's Hollow Road. Extra testing is being done. Preliminary results are expected by 20/04/2024.*

I would also like to raise a concern regarding the brutality of the attack at Black Water Farm. The farmer, aswell as all his livestock were slaughtered, with the primary suspect not looking like something human. Your input on this matter would be greatly appreciated.

Please let me know if there are additional details you require, or if there's anything else I can assist with regarding this case. I will ensure all updated documents are uploaded to the shared case file by the end of the day.

Thank you for your continued support.
Best regards,
Detective Inspector Rachel Morgan
Major Crimes Unit
Westbridge Police Department

GONE BEFORE THE MOON

Office: (01632) 478-214
Email: r.morgan@westbridgepd.gov'

What the hell! My fingers are shaking after reading the report. There is a farmer aswell as his livestock that's been killed at Black Water Farm. How can that be in any way connected to Kade? I can't tell if that means Kade's blood was found there? Or maybe someone else who was in both areas. I need to try and find a link to Kade and this farm, maybe there'll be something in his bedroom.

I tip toe along the upstairs hallway, trending carefully, making sure I don't make a sound along the wooden floorboards. I wince everytime I hear one of them creak. I can hear my Mum is now in her bedroom to the right of me, watching TV by the sound of it. I don't dare make another sound. My Mum hasn't seen me in Kade's room since he went missing, so I don't know how she is going to react. I can't risk her finding me.

I slowly turn the doorknob, releasing the door open. I slowly push it forwards, allowing myself to come into the room. Kade's room looks untouched, nothing being moved from the day he went missing. The posters on the walls stare down at me, their glossy surfaces catching the faint glow of the streetlight outside. It feels wrong to be in here without him. Like I am intruding. But I have to know.

I start with the obvious place to look, his desk drawers. They are a mess as always; pens without lids, crumpled receipts, a half-eaten, probably slightly mouldy granola bar shoved to the back. Nothing seems useful. I sift through his notebooks, but they are filled with the same chaotic sketches and half-finished ideas I've seen a hundred times before. I remember he wanted to have his own skateboard company. Designs to put on the skateboard decks are littered throughout the book.

The wardrobe is the next thing I check. I yank it open, a hoodie tumbles out onto the floor beside me. His clothes are crammed inside, barely hanging onto their hangers. I rummage through the pockets of his jackets and trousers, finding nothing but a few loose coins, an old movie ticket receipt, and a crumpled pack of gum. But no clues.

I kneel down beside his bed, glancing down into the darkness. The space is littered with old school books. There's also a shoebox, a bottle of vodka, and a few stray clothes. I pull them all out and pick up the shoebox to have a look. My heart sinks when I see pictures and birthday cards from his parents. He kept them all after they passed, a loving reminder of the joys they shared as a family. I can't help but shed a tear as I see this.

I look down at the bottle of vodka that I've pulled out. I've never drank before, but I'm really thinking it might be a good idea now. I unscrew the red cap and place it onto the floor next to me. The smell of it makes my face twist, but hell to it! I start to drink it, the head of the bottle touching my lips. The taste and strength of it hits me hard. I can only imagine this is what paint thinner tastes like; absolutely vile. And yet, I can't stop myself from taking another sip.

After a few minutes of drinking I calm myself down. Right, I have to try somewhere else, but where? I glance over to see a box in the corner of Kade's room. I stumble over and open it to see stuff from his old house, still unpacked. He'd been here a few months and still couldn't bear to fully unpack. Maybe he was wanting to go home, even though there was no home to go back to.

Frustration prickles me at the back of my neck. I sit back on my heels, trying to think. Where would Kade have hidden something important?

I look over to his bedside table where I see his laptop.

72

How could I be so stupid. Of course it's going to be there.

I hesitate for a moment before picking it up. Kade was paranoid about his privacy; I knew he wouldn't have left it unlocked. I plug in the charger, and after a few minutes I open the lid. The screen flickers to life and the desktop loads almost immediately. No password needed.

I can feel the alcohol start to hit me now and the screen starts to go fuzzy. Okay, where would it be now. I check through all the different folders on his hard drive, nervously wanting to see something that would stand out, but nothing. It's just school files and various drawings. There aren't any abnormalities at all. Email perhaps? Maybe he's been in contact with someone he shouldn't have been.

I open up his email account and again, nothing seems suspicious. I check the recently deleted folder, and to my surprise there's something there. An email from a company called Chimera Solutions. I open the email to have a look, the lines beginning to wave as I read it. It says:

'Dear Mr. Aston,

Thankyou for your recent enquiry into our biogenetic research operations, We are gravely sorry to hear about the passing of your parents. Whilst we knew of your parents requests for them to be involved in our research proceedings, unfortunately there are no openings at this current time for new enquiries. Should things change in the future, we will be in touch.

Best Regards,

Dr Stephen Heckingbottom, Executive Director of Human Innovation.'

What the hell is Chimera Solutions? Could this be related to Kade's disappearance? I can't help but feel like I'm onto something. I try to get up but stumble backwards, falling onto Kade's bed. I definitely drank way too much, it's taken a while to hit me. I thought I was fine to keep going but clearly not. I don't think I'm going to be much use at figuring this out tonight with my head spinning the way that it is. I'm going to rest here and go again in the morning.

TWELVE
Kade

The following item was taken into evidence at the scene after being found near the victims last whereabouts. The item was possessed by the Hearthwick Police Department and the results are as follows:

Type: Blood Sample
Blood Type: O positive
Match with victim: Yes
Type: Hair follicles
Colour: Dark Brown
Match with victim: Yes

- ***Forensic Report completed for Hearthwick Police Station — Tuesday, 15th April 2025***

"Well done, you seem to be adapting to the changes well. I see that you're growing stronger and stronger with each turn." A voice calls out.

I can't open my eyes to look. I try but they feel stapled shut, something holding them closed. I'm not too sure who is talking, but I assume it's the doctor.

"I feel great, I don't see why some of the fucks down here don't look and appreciate the hard work and vision. I'm stronger than ever, I don't think anyone can stop me." The rough voice has to be the Brute. I'd recognise his tone anywhere.

I try to move off the bed, but no matter how hard I try my body is failing to obey, my muscles lying there unresponsive. My limbs feel tied down with invisible weights that I can't seem to budge. I try to open my eyes again, my eyelids seem to betray me.

"What the hell is this?" I say, almost sounding shocked by the end of the sentence, maybe because of the fact that I'm actually able to get the words out.

"Well look who decided to wake up this time" mutters the Brute. "I bet you can't even remember what you did haha." His laugh angers me.

I feel he's just trying to get under my skin, and it's working. But what if he's not. What does he mean? What did I do? I haven't been awake since Carl and I tried to escape. Or have I? I can't help but go through every possibility. I feel a bit of unease in my heart.

"Stop now Slater! He's still coming around. He seems to have reacted slightly differently to the process than you. You're well over seven months into treatment, he's only just started" shouts the doctor, his anger fills the room.

I fight against the pain that's rushing through my body and mutter out a few more words "Stop it... Whatever you're doing... I... I can't... I can't... stop it..."

I can feel a deep heat sensation building in my chest, it's spreading outwards like a wildfire. I fall off the bed onto the floor, my body shaking uncontrollably. I feel like I'm going in and out of consciousness, as if it's a switch and someones standing next to it flipping it over and over again.

My eyes bolt open. I'm filled with rage and I don't know why. Everything feels red and I just want to kill. My body feels like it's growing, shifting as if it were made of playdough. My nails and teeth are growing, turning sharp on the ends.

I pull myself up and turn to look around, seeing a half broken mirror. What I see in the reflection is a monster, a monster not known in this world. The world around me has blurred, my senses overwhelmed. My hearing feels sharpened, catching sounds I've never noticed before. I'm losing touch with myself, I can't control my actions, maybe something else is. I feel like a pawn and someone's there with a remote control. Whatever it is, it's now in full control and I can't do anything about it. My thoughts and sights go black, falling into an abyss.

THIRTEEN
Duncan

I wake up to a pounding in my head, like a drumbeat that's out of sync with everything else. My eyes snap open, but the room still feels like it's spinning, as though I'm stuck on some carnival ride I didn't ask for. I blink, trying to focus on the ceiling, but it shifts and stretches, making me feel like I'm trapped in a slow-motion dream.

My mouth feels dry, as if my cotton balls have replaced my tongue. I still have a faint stale aftertaste of the vodka from last night. The light sifting through the window seems to blind me more than it should.

As I sit up I can feel my stomach trying to regurgitate yesterday's meals back up, it feels like it's doing backflips in my gut. I manage to stand, swaying like a zombie as I try to take a few steps. I've never been drunk before so I don't really know the procedure. I just know a glass of water right now would hit the spot.

I stumble down the stairs, grasping onto the handrail to keep me steady. I look into the kitchen to find my Mum making some porridge. The sweet smell of the honey she's drizzling on is a nice contrast to the stench of my alcohol filled breath that I can smell.

"You okay honey? You look a bit rough." My Mum's concerned voice questions my appearance.

78

"I'm okay, I just need some water. I drank some of Kade's vodka last night. I got a bit stressed." I feel like I am withholding enough information and it's burying me keeping it from her, the thought of getting something off my chest is nice. "I think I should be okay after a glass of water," I add.

She pauses, spoon halfway to the bowl, and turns to face me. Her eyes narrow, and I can already hear the sigh she's holding back.

"You drank what?" she asks, her voice calm, but laced with that unmistakable Mum disappointment.

I shift on my feet, suddenly more nauseous. "Vodka. Just a little," I mumble. "I was stressed."

She sets the spoon down with a quiet clink and crosses her arms. "Duncan, you're sixteen. You don't drink, and you definitely don't drink vodka." Her voice is firm, but there's something else there too… worry.

I look down at my hands. "I know. I just—" I hesitate, the words knotting in my throat. "Kade's missing, Mum. I don't know what to do."

Her expression softens, and she steps closer, resting a hand on my shoulder. "I get that you're scared, love. But drinking isn't going to bring him back."

I swallow hard. "I just wanted to forget for a bit."

She exhales, shaking her head before gently pulling me into a hug. "I know. But you don't have to do this alone, Duncan. We're going to find him. Together."

I nod against her shoulder, my headache momentarily forgotten.

I turn and gulp down some water, but it feels like it's not enough. The headache; that damn pounding doesn't ease up. I know this feeling is something that'll stick with me for the rest of the day, and I'm suddenly very aware of how unprepared I am for this. Never again, I think to myself, I know better.

I peek through one of the cupboards and take out two paracetamol. I've never been a fan of taking tablets so try to get them down in one big gulp.

I pull my phone out of my pocket and glance at it. There's a message sent twenty minutes ago from Aaron saying "Alright mate, any news on Kade? I still ain't heard anything." I remember the email now, reading it in my drunk state last night.

I turn to leave the kitchen and see my Mum side eyeing me, trying to make sure I'm okay. I carry on and go back upstairs and into my bedroom to log onto my computer. "Chimera Solutions, what could you be about then?" I say my thoughts aloud as I sit, hunched over my computer, my eyes burning from the flickering screen.

It is almost as if the search itself is taking longer than usual, like the very act of digging for the truth is resisting me. My fingers hover over the keyboard, restless. I can't shake the feeling that the answers are right there, just waiting to be uncovered. I scrolled through the search results for Chimera Solutions, hoping for a thread, something, anything, that would make sense of the vague hints I've picked up.

Chimera Solutions sounds so… clean, so professional. The company's website is sleek, boasting cutting-edge work in genetic research, with a focus on animal DNA. They speak about advancing science, about preserving endangered species, and about helping animals adapt to changing environments. It all seems perfectly legitimate on the surface.

There is something off about it. The nagging feeling in the back of my mind that won't go away, not since I'd learned they might be connected to Kade's disappearance. He's been in contact with them, regarding working with them. He hasn't been seen in nearly a week. I can't just sit here and hope it was a coincidence.

I dig deeper. One article mentions their latest projects, but it doesn't give much away. Ethical complaints, here and there, from animal rights activists and a few scientists, but nothing that stands out as truly concerning. Then, a link catches my eye: *'Chimera Solutions and the Ethical Boundaries of Genetic Engineering.'* It sounds promising. So I click.

The article is long, full of jargon, but I skim through it. The company has had its fair share of critics, accusations of pushing boundaries too far, even if most of it is theoretical. But none of it seems criminal. None of it explains what I needed to know about their involvement with Kade.

I lean back, rubbing my temples, frustrated. There has to be something more.

Then, just as I am about to close the tab, a name jumps out at me in an old forum comment. *'Dr. Magnus Blackthorne.'* It looks like a throwaway reference, tucked between the lines of a post that claimed the company has been involved in something shady, something hidden beneath the polished exterior. But there it is, a name. Blackthorne.

My curiosity flares. I open a new tab and type in his name, scanning through the search results. I see an old newspaper article from years ago. The headline makes my stomach drop. *'Scientist Exonerated in Animal Hybrid DNA Scandal.'*

Dr. Magnus Blackthorne had been accused of illegal testing. Hybrid DNA research involving both human and animal genes. The article outlines how he faced charges but had managed to avoid prison time after a technicality. It mentioned that the court ruled his experiments had *'no direct harm to living subjects,'* a loophole that has kept him free, despite protests from animal rights groups and others in the scientific community.

81

I keep searching, opening new tabs, looking through old news stories and reports. Finally, buried deep in the results, I find an address. Chimera Solutions has a headquarters in Eldermere. It's a big city about thirty minutes by car from where I am now.

I sit back in my chair, steadying my breathing as I stare at the screen. This is it. The lead I've been searching for. It wasn't much, just a couple of names and a location, but it's a start. Enough to make me finally stand up, grab my jacket, and head out the door. I can't keep digging through endless pages of information. I need answers, and I am going to get them, one way or another.

FOURTEEN
Duncan

Day 3 of treatment. The new subject appears to be adapting well, showing no signs of failure and his body adapting to the procedure well. I will up proceedings tomorrow, seeing how he'll react.

- **Medical journal entry from Dr. Magnus Blackthorne — Tuesday, 15th April 2025**

"May I have your attention, please? The 10:52 service to Eldermere is now departing from Platform 3. Calling at Westmarch, Frostwick, Fenwick Hollows and Clagshaw. Please ensure you have all your belongings with you before boarding. Stand clear of the doors and mind the gap between the train and the platform. Thank you for traveling with Pennyfare Rail, and we wish you a pleasant journey." The rusted old tannoy system barks the message across the station.

Only me and a few other people aboard the train. I get in the middle of the three carriages, meaning I'm able to see down both sides, in case a ticket inspector comes. I don't have any money at the moment, so I have to try and chance a free ride, something I wouldn't normally do.

The carriage sways slightly as we make our way out of town, passing by agricultural fields that lie either side of the track. The train should only take around thirty minutes to get to

83

Eldermere. From there I don't know how to get to Chimera Solutions headquarters, but I'm sure if I ask the right people they'll be able to point me in the right direction.

There's only a few other passengers scattered about the carriage, some lost in their own thoughts, others staring out of the windows. The soft clink of the occasional door opening keeps panicking me, expecting the ticket officer to emerge from the doorway. It does break the silence now and then, but overall, it feels peaceful.

I glance around. A newspaper rests folded on the lap of an older man sitting across the aisle, his tired eyes drifting between the page and the view outside. Another woman that I can see further up the carriage has her headphones in, swaying to the sound of the music.

"We are now approaching Westmarch. Please ensure you have all your belongings with you before departing. Stand clear of the doors and mind the gap between the train and the platform. Thank you for traveling with Pennyfare Rail, and we wish you a pleasant journey." The woman with her headphones departs onto the platform, and four more people hop on, spreading themselves throughout the carriage.

As we begin to take off again I peer towards the front of the train. The ticket inspector is making his way down. My heart starts to race, my palms begin to sweat. I've got no ticket.

He enters my carriage, to which I'm seated about half way down. The officer moves steadily, a figure of authority in his crisp uniform, his eyes are scanning the passengers with a quiet focus. I don't want to make eye contact; I don't want to give anything away. I sit a little straighter, trying to act casual, but it's like the world's spotlight is now trained on me.

I scan the carriage for any way out. Behind me there's a toilet. It's the most obvious place to hide, but I've got no choice. If he finds me without a ticket I'll be thrown off at the next stop, too far to walk to Eldermere.

Without thinking anymore about it I stand, trying to calmly move out of my seat and down the corridor. I glance back and see that he hasn't noticed me.

As I reach the door, I slip inside the cramped toilet, the faint scent of disinfectant fills the air. I lock the door with a slight shake of my hand, pressing my back against the cool wall, my breath shallow. The sound of the officer's footsteps grows closer. I can almost hear the shuffle of his uniform as he stops at the seat next to mine, unaware that I've just slipped into this tiny, claustrophobic space, hidden away from view.

The footsteps are passing by the toilet, not stopping to check. Is this it? Have I done it?

I wait another minute until they are fully gone and make my way cautiously back to my seat. As I turn, I jump, the ticket officer is there.

"Thought you could sneak away that easily?" He chuckles.

The ticket officer is a middle-aged man with greying hair at the temples, a sharp jawline, and dark, calculating eyes. His uniform is neat and crisp, the badge gleaming on his chest. He carries himself with quiet authority. He doesn't look like the kind of guy that's going to let me off.

"Sorry... I think I've lost it..." I say with a stuttering voice, not nearly convincing enough.

"Look kid, you can't just be getting free rides, I'm gonna have to tell you to get off at the next stop, unless you want to purchase a ticket?" His voice is firm and commanding.

I don't really know what to say, I have to get there, maybe I can guilt trip him. "I'm sorry... Look, I'm going to be honest, I don't have any money. My friend has gone missing and I'm trying to find him. I've got a lead that he might be in Eldermere." The last bit was a bit of a lie but I have to make it

85

sound more plausible than just chasing some half hearted lead.

"Is that one of the people on the news, the mystery about all of the disappearances that have happened recently?" He seems intrigued.

I reply "Yes, look I don't know for definite if he's there, but I have to try, the police haven't come up with anything and I'm desperate."

He looks into my eyes, judging whether I'm being truthful. "Look, I don't normally do this, but just this once I'll let you off. I've got a family friend who knows someone that's missing. The unknown is the biggest killer." He says, his voice slightly crackling as he speaks. "Here, here's a return ticket. I hope you find your friend," he adds, handing me a ticket.

"Thank you... that's so kind..." I don't know how to react. I guess with all the stress I have forgotten about the kindness of strangers.

As the officer walks off, I sit there, staring out into the passing scenery, wondering what on earth I'm going to say when I enter Chimera Solutions.

As I get off the train, Eldemere station is spotless, a complete contrast to Hearthwick. The slight smell of oil from the tracks is the only foul thing in the area. That is to be expected though, it is a train station after all.

The carriage had got a lot busier towards the end of my journey, nearly an extra one hundred people climbed onto the carriages at Fenwick Hallows and a few extra at Clagshaw. They are all getting off now, Eldemere seems to be the destination for everyone today.

I walk with the big flow of people that are making their way through the station, heading up the stairs to the exit. I'm being careful not to fall, tripping here would mean getting trampled on by the ongoing herd. Everyone is shoulder to shoulder, like sardines. I can't help but pull a face at the smell of body odor coming from the person next to me. Hygiene seems to go amiss with some people by the seams of it. The station is underground so there is no fresh air to disperse any of the stench.

As I walk I can see various displays, littered along the wall with different train routes, lit up by an array of colours signalling key stops. A few different pictures of the surrounding towns are incorporated in the display. They don't have any of Hearthwick, mind I can't blame them. One quick peep of that place would be enough to turn most people away.

The crowd disperses as we emerge from up the stairs, into the streets of Eldemere, the fresh air a nice change from the congested mix of smells coming from other passengers. This city is full of life, skyscraper buildings fill either side of the high street, with multi story historical buildings adding a nice sense of history and culture with the modern architecture. Cars are parked along the side that we have emerged from, a mix of taxis and public cars, ready to give lifts to the train users.

I'm not sure how far this headquarters is. I would have checked on my phone but my mobile data ran out yesterday. Do I ask around? Or shall I find a place with free wifi? This place is completely unknown and a lot of the people look quite intimidating.

I start to stroll down the road, to where there looks to be a shopping center, I can see the large M of a McDonalds signalled inside. They always have free wifi so I should check there.

As I'm walking, I can't help but feel anxious, the unknown is driving me crazy. I usually try to avoid places like this, where there are loads of people. I feel like they're all watching me, eyes pinging me from all across the street.

The shopping center looks quite big. Luckily, the

McDonalds is right near the start of it. I walk up to the window and pull out my phone, searching for nearby wifi signals. *'The Cloud'* pops up so I click it. This is the wifi they use all over the country, all you need to do is sign in. It's quite slow but eventually it connects. I type the address in on Google Maps and look. After a few seconds I start to worry, the time dragging on feels longer than it should.

"Come on, work… Bloody thing" I say out loud.

"Struggling for a signal? These silly new phones are rubbish" laughs an elderly woman as she passes, hearing my frustration. I can't help but let out a small giggle at her comment.

My phone doesn't work so I put it back in my pocket, frustrated yet worried. I walk back onto the high street. I guess I'll have to do this the old fashioned way.

I scan the street, looking for someone who seems… approachable? Whatever that means. Most people are walking with too much purpose for me to approach them. I have to find someone that looks like they can help. My pulse quickens as I lock onto a middle-aged guy standing near a coffee shop a few buildings down, scrolling through his phone. Okay. This is fine. Just ask.

I shuffle up, clearing my throat. "Uh, excuse me?" My voice comes out weirdly quiet. I hate this sort of stuff.

The guy looks up, polite but mildly confused. "Yeah?"

I swallow hard. "Do you, um, know where ummm… Chimera Solutions is?"

His brow furrows. "Chimera Solutions?" He glances around like the answer might magically appear before pulling out his phone. "Let me check." The wait feels endless. I shift on my feet, resisting the urge to just bolt and figure it out myself.

He nods. "Yeah, looks like it's just down that street,

second left, then the next right and it should be right there." He points, and I follow his gesture with my eyes, committing it to memory.

"Oh. Okay. Thanks." I barely wait for his nod before I'm already walking away, heart still hammering. At least it's all over. If I'm anywhere near this nervous, I'm going to get nowhere. I have to compose myself.

FIFTEEN
Duncan

Nestled within the heart of the city, the Chimera Solutions headquarters stands as an unassuming yet sophisticated structure, seamlessly integrated into the modern urban landscape. At first glance, it appears like any other contemporary office building. Its sleek glass façade reflects the ever-changing sky, steel accents lending it a crisp, professional aesthetic. Yet, a closer look reveals the subtle design choices that whisper of the company's unique purpose.

The building is mid-rise, about ten stories tall, with clean, angular lines softened by vertical gardens that climb sections of its exterior. The entrance is understated, a set of revolving glass doors framed by polished stone, above which, a modest yet elegant logo. It's a stylized DNA helix intertwined with animal motifs etched into the metal canopy. What looks to be a green rooftop terrace, barely visible from street level, provides a hint of the company's commitment to nature and biotechnology, while narrow, tinted windows punctuate the structure, giving it a slightly enigmatic presence.

I am completely taken back by the beauty of the architecture. I'm nervous to go into such a built up piece, but I swallow my fears and make my way through the revolving doors.

Inside, the reception exudes a quiet efficiency. The

floor is polished concrete, cool beneath my feet, while the walls feature embedded LED panels that display shifting, abstract patterns reminiscent of cellular structures. A subtle hum of activity permeates the air. Researchers in crisp lab coats are passing through security checkpoints on the far side of the lobby, their access badges flashing under discreet scanners. I can also see a few office staff moving between glass-walled conference rooms, probably engaging in quiet discussions.

I walk cautiously towards the reception desk. The air inside is cool, almost clinically so, carrying the faint scent of coffee. A fairly young woman is sitting at the reception, writing something down, her head almost buried beneath the desk. She looks up from her monitor as I approach, her dark hair is pulled back into a neat ponytail.

"Good afternoon," she says smoothly, her voice carrying the practiced warmth of someone used to greeting strangers all day. "Welcome to Chimera Solutions. How can I help you?"

"H… Hello?" I ask, unsure of how to open my inquiry. I swallow, forcing a calm expression. I can't afford to say too much about the situation, not yet. "I'm here to see Dr. Stephen Heckingbottom," I add, keeping my voice level. "The Executive Director of Human Innovation here at Chimera Solutions."

Her eyes flicker with something. Curiosity, maybe, but she doesn't question me. Instead, she types something into her computer, the quiet tapping of keys filling the momentary silence.

"Are you one of the apprentices? Do you have an appointment?" she asks, glancing up confused.

"No, I'm not an apprentice, and no I don't have an appointment, but it's important," I reply, offering a carefully neutral smile. "I was hoping he might be available for a few minutes."

She hesitates, her fingers hovering over the keyboard. This is the part where she decides whether to dismiss me outright or escalate my request. I keep my stance relaxed, but my pulse is quickening. If they turn me away, I'll have to find another way in.

"I'll check," she says finally, picking up the phone. As she dials, I glance around the lobby again, scanning for anything; any sign, any clue that might tell me if I'm in the right place. My friend is missing, and everything has led me here. But whether that means help or danger, I haven't figured out yet.

The receptionist murmurs something into the receiver, then looks back at me, her expression giving nothing away. "Dr. Heckingbottom's office will get back to me in a moment" she says, setting the phone down. "You're welcome to wait."

I nod and step back, forcing myself to breathe evenly. This is just the beginning. One way or another, I will find out what happened and who I can trust.

"I'm just going to pop to the loo if that's okay?" I need to compose myself somewhere private, get my shit together for a second.

She points to the right. "Just down there and on the left."

"Thankyou" I reply, beginning my scurry to the toilet.

I make my way across the lobby, keeping my steps measured and unhurried, though my mind is racing. I spot the bathroom sign near the far wall, past a sleek seating area where employees tap away at tablets and sip coffee from branded mugs. Pushing the door open, I step inside.

The bathroom is spotless, the kind of place designed to be forgotten, neutral grey tiles, recessed lighting, the faint scent of citrus-scented cleaner lingering in the air. I move past the row of sinks and into a stall, closing the door behind me with a quiet click.

I exhale slowly, leaning against the cool metal divider. I need a moment. Just a second to collect myself, to push down the gnawing uncertainty twisting in my stomach. My friend is missing. Chimera Solutions is my only lead. And I just walked into the lion's den without a plan.

Before I can settle, the door swings open. Footsteps, two of them. I stay perfectly still, barely breathing as two voices break the silence.

"I'm telling you, it's weird. This thing with the hack? It's too specific," one says. It's a man, his tone is low, but edged with irritation.

"Yeah, I don't like it," the second voice replies. It sounds like a younger man, his voice a bit higher pitched. "Someone's been poking around in our files and emails. It's not random. They're looking for something." My heartbeat stumbles.

The first man sighs. "Security's already sweeping the system, but if it's an inside job—"

"Or an outsider," he cuts in. A pause. Then, in a quieter voice: "What about Blackthone? Or Chesterfield? Hell it could have been any of the previous employees."

Blackthorne? His name popped up before when I was searching about this place. I can't help but feel he might somehow be connected to all this.

Silence stretches between them, thick with unspoken suspicion. Then, the sharp sound of a paper towel ripping from the dispenser, the crumple of fabric. One of them exhales, irritated.

"Let's just be careful," one of the men mutters. "Last thing we need is some guy getting all our data. There was also that visitor just now, reception didn't say much, but we should keep an eye out." My stomach tightens.

The other man cuts in. "He was just a kid, man. Doubt he's hacking us. Most likely one of those animal rights activists we occasionally get."

A moment later, the door swings open again, and their voices fade down the hall. I stay frozen for a few more seconds, heart pounding. They weren't talking about me were they? Not yet surely. Maybe someone else has already drawn attention to this place, and if I'm not careful, I'll be next.

Taking a slow, measured breath, I step out of the stall. At the sinks, I turn on the tap, letting the cold water run over my hands before splashing some onto my face. The chill steadies me, just enough to force my expression into something neutral again.

I dry off, square my shoulders, and step back into the lobby. The receptionist glances up as I approach, offering the same professional smile. I return it, pretending I didn't just overhear something I shouldn't have. Now I really need to see Dr. Heckingbottom.

"Unfortunately Dr. Heckingbottom's schedule is very busy today, he currently doesn't have any time for unscheduled meetings or chats, is there a message I can pass onto him?" the receptionist explains, her professional smile almost feeling like a gloat.

I exhale sharply through my nose. A message? No, that's not going to work. I hit back with "I appreciate that, but this is something I need to tell him in person." I can't help but feel like my tone sounds a tad aggressive in reply.

"I understand, but if you could just tell me what it's about. If you need help with class projects or something like that then you'd be wasting your time. I'd suggest going to the library and getting one of the textbooks." she says, but she doesn't understand. She just wants me to leave. "I'll make sure your message reaches the appropriate team if you tell me."

"No, listen..." I step in slightly. "This isn't some casual request, I have to tell him in person, trust me, he needs to hear this face to face."

She doesn't budge, not even blinking. She's staring right through me, I feel as though she is debating calling over security. "I'm sorry but Dr. Heckingbottom is unavailable, I can't change his schedule, even if I wanted to."

I glance around and see two security guards, watching over at me from a distance. I have to be careful not to get kicked out, but I have to see him. I place my hands on the desk. "Look, I don't want any trouble. It's just I have to speak to him, trust me, he's going to want to hear what I say."

"Look, I can't do anything about his schedule, I've already told you" her voice raises.

I slam my fist on the desk, completely against what I'd usually do in this situation, but my blood is boiling. I hear the footsteps of the security guards approaching behind me, they're walking towards me with pace.

"I think it's best you leave sir" says one of the guards, grabbing me by the shoulder.

"Look, I need to see him, why won't you listen?"

The other security guard grabs me by the shoulder aswell, both of them pulling me backwards quickly, making my head snap back with the force. I'm being pulled out, I have to try something. What can get me in? Surely there's something I can say? There's got to be.... the hack. That's my way in.

With my feet dragging beneath me, I'm nearly out the door. I'm still facing the reception desk, the receptionist is just watching me get kicked out. "It's about the hack! I have information on the hack!" I shout.

The guards stop in their tracks, the woman's face looks shocked. "I'm sorry did you just say you had information on the hack? Let me just make a call. Wait there." The receptionist suddenly seems interested in my story. It was a bit of a white lie, but I had to do something. I've got a feeling this hack might be related to Kade's disappearance. Well, I don't know, but I'm clutching at straws.

The woman dials on the phone and murmurs something into it, she seems in a rush. "Room 14B, you've got 5 minutes." She says.

It worked, but now I have to go in there, not knowing any information on this so-called hack, but pretending to, so that I can get information on Kade.

The receptionist barely glances up as I'm finally given access beyond the reception. One of the security guards, broad-shouldered, expressionless, steps in beside me, a silent escort. No words are exchanged. Just a nod toward the path I'm now expected to follow.

We head to the right of the reception desk, where there is a set of frosted glass doors, sleek and silent as they slide open. The transition is immediate.

As we go through the doors, we approach a stairwell, no ordinary one. Unlike the usual industrial metal and concrete designs, these stairs are sculpted from polished steel and reinforced glass, wrapping in a smooth, controlled spiral that goes up to the upper levels of the building. A thin LED strip glows along the edges of each step, casting a cold blue light that makes everything feel clinical. No scuff marks. No signs of wear. It feels like no one walks these stairs unless they have to.

At the top, the hallways stretch out in opposite directions, both eerily identical. Smooth white floors, subtle lighting embedded in the ceiling, and walls so seamless they look molded rather than built. It's unnerving. There are no decorations, no windows, no signs of human presence beyond the occasional security camera nestled into the corners, tracking every step.

I follow the guard down the right-hand corridor, my footsteps barely making a sound against the synthetic flooring. Doors line the hallway, each one matte black with a small, illuminated name plate beside it. This room reads '14B'. There's no handles on the doors, just keycard scanners aswell as a built-in panel displaying a holographic interface. No indication of what lies beyond each one. Research labs? Offices? Something else entirely?

The guard pulls out his ID card, scanning it on the keycard scanner. There is a small red light that flickers onto the keycard before a little chime rings out, confirming our access into the room. The doors hiss open.

Inside, the room is just as cold and calculated as the rest of the facility. A long, glass-top conference table sits in the center, lined with ergonomic chairs that look designed for function, not comfort. A digital display covers one wall, a faint pulse of blue light running through it as it idles.

I step inside, and the door seals shut behind me. This isn't just going to be a meeting. This is going to be an interrogation.

After only a few moments of waiting, the doors open again. A man walks in. From first impressions, I can only describe him as having the look of a figure of calculated brilliance wrapped in a sleek, high-tech lab coat. Silver streaks run through his unkempt hair. His sharp, intelligent eyes scan a holographic interface projected from his sleeve, before they switch to me, restless, relentless, almost as if he's staring at me under a microscope. This has to be him, this has to be Dr. Heckingbottom.

As he places his tablet on the table he says "You claimed Chimera Solutions was being hacked." His voice is sharp, clipped. "You have five minutes kid."

97

I swallow. I expected hostility, but not this level of indifference. "Right. Uh, I…" I clear my throat. "I have reason to believe someone's been in your system. Accessing emails. I don't know the details, but—"

"Then why are you here?" His fingers tap once against the table, impatient. "If you don't have evidence, you're wasting my time."

I grit my teeth. He's trying to push me off balance, and I can't let him. "Look, I wouldn't have come here if this wasn't serious. My friend, Kade, reached out to this company about volunteering for some kind of research. And now, he's missing."

Something shifts in Heckingbottom's expression, so brief I almost miss it. A flicker of recognition? Annoyance? It's gone before I can place it.

"People go missing for all kinds of reasons. Why would that have anything to do with us?" He snaps back.

"Because someone saw his email. Someone with access. And that someone took him." I lean forward, lowering my voice. "You and I both know your security isn't as airtight as you'd like to believe."

The room goes silent for a moment. Heckingbottom exhales sharply through his nose, adjusting his glasses. "What exactly are you implying?"

I hesitate. Push too hard, and he'll shut this down; but if I don't push at all, I walk out of here with nothing. "I think an ex-employee is involved. Maybe one with a grudge. Someone who knows how to get into your system." I watch his face carefully. "Maybe someone like… Dr. Blackthorne?"

This time, the reaction is real. It's subtle, his fingers tighten around the tablet for half a second, but it's there. "Dr. Blackthorne is no longer with this company." His words are deliberate, final.

98

"But he was. And if he still has access—"

"He does not have access," Heckingbottom cuts in, his voice like ice.

"Then why do you look nervous?" I snap back.

His jaw tightens. He stands abruptly, picking up his tablet. "This meeting is over."

"Wait—"

"You're grasping at shadows, Mr. Duncan. Your friend's disappearance has nothing to do with us. And if you falsely claim otherwise, I will ensure legal action is taken. I suggest you get back to school and stop this witch hunt that you seem to be on."

I clench my fists under the table. He's lying. Maybe not directly, but he knows something. "You don't even care, do you?" I say, standing. "A kid is missing. And you're more worried about your company's reputation."

Heckingbottom gives me a cold, detached look. "I care about facts. And the fact is, you no longer have a reason to be in this building."

The door hisses open behind him. Security is waiting. I walk past Dr. Heckingbottom to leave, but just as I reach the doorway, he speaks again.

"Mr. Duncan." I pause. "Some doors are locked for a reason. Don't make the mistake of forcing one open."

I don't respond. I just walk out. But I've got what I need. He knows something. And if Dr. Blackthorne is involved, I'm going to find out exactly what he's hiding.

SIXTEEN
Marlon

The voices in my head are getting worse. I'm not sure if I'm going crazy or if that sick bastard did something to me. My thoughts are so loud it's giving me headaches, I can't even control what I'm thinking.

- ***Unknown Journal entry — Tuesday, 15th April 2025***

I push open the heavy wooden door of The King's Arms, and the warmth of the place hits me immediately; the low hum of conversation, the scent of beer and something fried hanging in the air. It's a proper old-school pub, the kind with worn wooden beams and a landlord who's seen it all.

Beside me, Gordon lets out a long sigh, rolling his shoulders back, like he's finally shaking off the weight of the shift. It feels weird thinking of him as Gordon now, rather than PC Churchill. The professional standards of the police make it always seem like he's more of a colleague than a friend. Not that he is the usual kind that I hang out with in my spare time, but deep down I feel like his heart is in the right place, and I can't fault that.

"Christ, I need a pint," Gordon mutters, already making a beeline for the bar.

I follow, feeling lighter now that we're out of uniform. I swapped mine for a plain white T-shirt and some jeans, but

Gordon still looks like a cop, even in an old checkered buttoned-up shirt, trousers that scream 'dad at a barbecue,' and that same authoritative stance that makes people instinctively behave around him.

Behind the bar, Moira gives us a knowing look. "The usual, lads?" she asks, already reaching for the taps.

"Please," I say, leaning against the counter.

She slides Gordon his bitter first, he grunts his thanks and then hands me my lager. I take a slow sip, letting the cold fizz wash away the taste of stale coffee and stress.

"You young ones don't know how to enjoy a proper drink," Gordon grumbles, eyeing my pint. "That's piss compared to a proper ale."

I smirk. "Maybe I just don't like drinking something that tastes like a loaf of bread."

He scoffs but doesn't argue, taking a long pull from his glass.

The pub carries on around us, there are old blokes nursing pints, a group of mates laughing over a game of darts and the occasional glance in our direction, but nothing hostile. It's a local's place, the kind where you earn your welcome over time. And despite everything, I think we have. It's become a bit of a tradition over the past couple of months that I've been partnered with Gordon. To go out for a drink once a week after work.

I let out a breath I didn't realise I was holding. The job is still waiting for us tomorrow. But for now? It's just me, Gordon, and a couple of well-earned pints.

"Did you hear back off that dentist Gords" I snicker as I speak.

"For fuck sake man!" Gordon shoots me a look of annoyance with a slight smirk as he's speaking. "No Gords, No Gordinator, No G Dog, It's Gordon. I don't know how many times I have to tell you."

I can't help but laugh, I know he's hating it since I've been giving him some silly nicknames, but I can't help but do it. "Okay, I'm sorry... So... did she reply?"

"She did, supposed to be meeting her the weekend for a drink." He replies.

A smile creeps onto my face. "Let's go man, I told you she was into you. You've gotta tell her some of your old stories that you told me the other day, she'll love them."

"I've got more to tell, some of them more crazy than the ones I said the other day."

"Go on" I say.

Gordon takes a slow sip of his pint, smacking his lips like he's about to impart some great wisdom. "Right," he says, leaning in slightly. "Let me tell you about the time I arrested a bloke with a goat."

I raise an eyebrow. "A goat?"

"A bloody goat," he confirms, shaking his head. "Back in the nineties, I was working a late shift in Brixton. We get a call. Some fella's running down the High Street, stark bollock naked, carrying a goat under his arm. Now, you'd think that's the weird bit. But no. Turns out, the goat was also wearing a bra."

I nearly spit out my drink. "You're joking."

"Wish I was." He takes another sip. "We had to chase him round the whole town trying to get this bloody goat off him and bring him in."

"Crazy, I want to be able to tell stories like that. Seems the most crazy thing at the moment is that stuff that's going on with the meteor and the rocket ship, did you hear about that?"

"I saw something on the news about that, what happened." Gordon replies.

I take another sip of my lager. "So these scientists

thought they possibly found some kind of alien life on this meteor. They went to bring it in and there was some big explosion, killing them all. No-one knows what happened to the meteor either, some reckon it's heading for earth, I even saw some people saying it's going to its home planet. I think they're all a load of whackos."

Gordon scratches his head. "It's a weird place we're in right now, It's like—"

Gordon's interrupted as his phone buzzes against the wooden table. He barely glances at it before sighing.

"Bloody hell," he mutters, setting his pint down and picking up his mobile from in front of him. "Never a quiet night, is it?"

I take a sip of my lager as he answers. "Churchill."

For a moment he goes silent, I know something is wrong. His expression shifts, eyebrows knitting together, jaw tightening. The usual gruff indifference gives way to something sharper. Urgent.

"...What could even do that?" His voice drops, but the pub is noisy enough that no one else notices. I lean in slightly.

A beat of silence, then he lets out a breath. "You're having a laugh."

Another pause. His grip on the phone tightens.

"Right. I'll be there in ten." He hangs up and immediately reaches for his coat.

"What's going on?" I ask, already feeling that familiar pull of duty creeping back in.

He throws some cash on the table, not even waiting for his change. "There's a bloody massacre going on in the city. Like what happened at Black Water Farm."

I blink. "...A massacre?"

"Yep." He shoves his arms through his jacket. "And something's attacking people. They don't know what it is."

103

For a second, I thought he was winding me up. But the look on his face says otherwise.

I down the last of my pint, wipe my mouth, and grab my own coat. "Right then." I say, standing up. "Let's go sort this shit out."

SEVENTEEN
Marlon

PC Churchill's car jerks to a stop, tires screeching against the rain-slick pavement. I barely have time to unbuckle my seatbelt before the radio crackles with another panicked report. More civilians down, structural damage, and something big still on the move. It's going to make this even harder with the rain and the sun beginning to go down.

I step out of the car, my boots splashing into a puddle tinged pink with blood. The street ahead is like a warzone. A row of parked cars lay mangled like discarded tin cans, windows smashed in, metal twisted by something with brute force. A lamppost has been torn clean from its base, sparking where it had fallen onto a wrecked van. Shattered glass litters the ground, and the air reeks of petrol, burnt rubber, and something... feral.

PC Churchill whistles low under his breath as he joins me, sweeping his torch across the carnage. "What the hell did this? A tank?"

Some people that were at the scene before us are mutilated on the cold ground, their bodies unrecognisable.

"No tank leaves claw marks that deep." I point to the side of a butcher's shop where long, ragged gashes have been carved into the brick. The sign above the door dangled by one remaining bolt, swaying ominously in the wind.

A wet groan sounds from our right. A man lies half-pinned beneath an overturned motorbike, his face pale and bloodied. I rush over, lifting the weight off him while PC Churchill checks his injuries. "What happened here? What did you see?"

The man's breath comes in ragged gasps. "It was... it was massive. It's a bear—" He winces "But not right... not normal..."

"Might be the thing that caused the massacre at Black Water Farm." I mutter.

Before I can ask more, a deep, guttural snarl echoes through the narrow street. We both snap our heads towards the sound. Just beyond the wreckage, past the alley where the streetlights flicker weakly, something shifts. A hulking shadow looms between the ruined remains of two cars, steam rising from its matted fur in the cold night air. Then, two glowing amber eyes lock onto us.

PC Churchill exhales sharply, reaching for his taser. "Tell me that's just a very pissed-off zoo escapee."

The beast takes a slow step forward, claws clicking against the pavement. I don't answer his question. I just reach for my baton, heart hammering. The bear is bigger than the two cars combined, with each step closer, it becomes bigger and bigger, towering over everything in its way. I'm frozen, I can't move because of the fear.

"That's got to be the biggest bear I've ever seen. It's got to be fifteen feet high when standing on its back legs."

"Marlon, let's worry less about measuring it, and more about getting to safety. When I count down from three, go into that building. I'll keep the thing distracted." PC Churchill whispers, nodding towards the butchers.

"But what about you?" I reply, being cautious not to be too loud.

106

"It's going to go for something, so I'll stay, you go."
This is the first time I've ever heard fear in his voice. "Three,
two, one, go."

I slowly back off, walking backwards towards the
butchers behind us. I step through the big, broken glass
window. I trip up on the window frame and fall to the ground,
cutting myself on the shards of glass as I hit the ground.

I crawl backwards around the counter and press my
back against it, my breath coming fast and shallow. The cold
tiles beneath my shoes and hands are slick with something that
I don't want to think about. The air has a stench of raw meat
mixed with blood. I can hear heavy footfalls; fast and pounding
against the pavement like a sledgehammer.

I risk a glance through the shattered window. The beast
is charging. It's moving with terrifying speed, its massive
frame forms a blur of dark fur and muscle as it tears across the
street. The glow of the streetlights catches its massive
shoulders, each step making the ground tremble. Churchill
barely has time to react. He raises his taser, but the thing is
already on him.

A deep, guttural roar shakes the air as the bear collides
with him like a freight train. Churchill's body is lifted clean off
the ground, hurling backward into the crumpled remains of a
car. The impact crunches metal and shatters glass, and he
slumps against the hood, motionless.

Shit. I clench my baton tighter, every instinct
screaming at me to do something. What the hell can I do? The
taser barely had a chance. My baton? Useless. My radio?
Who's going to get here in time?

The beast looms over Churchill, breath steaming in the
cold night air. Its claws flexed, glinting in the dim light, and
then, its head snaps up. It sniffs.

I duck lower behind the counter, my pulse hammering

in my throat. It knows I am here. The beast's footsteps grow louder and quicker, closing in on the butcher's shop. The walls shake as it crashes through the front of the shop, its massive frame ripping through the remains of the door like paper. Splinters and glass rain down, and I barely have time to duck back down behind cover before one of his claws swipe where my head was just a second ago.

I hit the ground hard, knocking the wind out of my lungs. My baton is gone, useless anyway. I must have dropped it in my panic. I find something better; a butcher's cleaver, thick and heavy, still with the remnants of whatever the last cut had been.

The bear lets out a deep, rattling growl, its breath steaming as it exhales. My mind is screaming at me to run, but I hold my ground. If I bolt, it will be on me in an instant.

It sniffs the air, the beast's eerie yellow eyes sweeping across the wreckage, looking for me. It's fur dripping in blood. Churchill's blood? Someone else's? It doesn't matter, it'll be mine if I don't survive this.

The bear lunges at me. I barely get the cleaver up in time, the blade biting into its shoulder, cutting through thick muscle. It roars, louder than anything I'd ever heard, saliva spitting from its mouth, shooting across my face.

I try to get to my feet as it swipes at me again, with a paw the size of my chest. Pain explodes out of my side as I'm flung backwards, crashing into a glass display case. The sharp shards dig deep into my back, tearing through my t-shirt and biting into my skin. I gasp, gripping my side. Hot sticky blood soaking through my white shirt, making it look like a bad tie dye attempt.

The bear doesn't give me a chance to recover. It charges again. I grab a fistfull of broken glass, ignoring the sting as the edges slice into my fingers. I hurl it into the beast's face. It rears back with a snarl, shaking its head, momentarily blinded. I take my chance, dragging myself to my feet and stumbling into the backroom.

My left arm throbs with a deep gash running from my shoulder to my forearm. But I don't stop, I can't. I need a weapon, a place to hide, or some sort of exit route.

I pass through some curtains and into a walk-in meat locker. Hanging carcasses fill the room. I notice a large number of cabinets and storage spaces in the room. I shove myself into one of them, about half way into the room. There is no handle on the inside so I am gripping onto a small latch, hoping my sweaty hands can maintain a good enough grip to keep it closed.

The bear makes its way through the doorway, barely squeezing through the gap. I clamp my spare hand over my mouth, chest heaving.

It stalks forward, sniffing, growling low through its throat. The floor freaks with its weight. Every step makes my heart skip a bit.

I start to lose grip on the latch, my hands slipping off it. The door creaks open and the bear turns to look.

I grit my teeth, sweat mixing with the blood and glass shards splattered across my face. I've got one chance, this is it.

The bear turns its head away for a split second. I burst out from the cupboard, grabbing a meat hook from the wall behind me. I lunge forward and swing it with everything I've got. The sharp edge digs into the bear's side, making it roar in fury. I twist it in further before yanking it free, sending blood spraying across the room.

It's not enough. The bear lashes out, claws raking across my side. My vision flashes white with pain. My legs give out and I crash onto my back, gasping for breath.

I am done. Then—Gunfire.

109

The front of the butchers shop erupts with noise as armed police officers storm in, rifles barking. The bear roars and rears up, its massive form is silhouetted by muzzle flashes. Bullets tear into its thick hide, forcing it backwards.

It turns, giving me one last growl, then spins on its feet and crashes through the brick wall, disappearing into the wooded area beyond.

I cough, spitting blood onto the floor. A shadow looms over me. It's one of the officers. "Jesus Christ, he's alive! Medic!"

I let my head fall back again, against the cold hard tiles, chest rising and falling in shallow breaths. The bear is gone, for now.

EIGHTEEN
Marlon

"Madness!!! There was a bear attack in Ravenwood today! That's only about thirty minutes away! Didn't look like some ordinary bear though, it was like twice the size. Knew the day would come when things would pop off like this. Wish I could have been the one to save the day though :("
- ***Online Blog entry from Milton Fizzlewick — Wednesday, 16th April 2025***

I wake to the steady beep of a heart monitor and the sharp, sterile smell of disinfectant. My body aches like it's been hit by a freight train. Considering last night, it wasn't far from the truth. My arm and side throbs, a dull, pulsing pain that goes beneath layers of bandages.

Fluorescent lights buzz softly overhead, white walls surround me, a curtain drawn halfway around the bed, yeah this is a hospital.

For a moment, I just lie there, staring at the ceiling, my mind feels sluggish. It starts to all come rushing back. The bear, the fight, the gunfire… Churchill.

I turn my head too fast, pain flaring in my ribs as I try to sit up. A grunt escapes my throat. The movement draws someone's attention. It's an officer in uniform, standing near the doorway. DC Emily Langford. She has a serious expression, her arms crossed.

She steps closer. "Marlon. You're awake."

"Churchill," I rasp, my throat dry as sandpaper. "Where is he?"

She doesn't answer right away. The pause, the hesitation, it tells me everything before she even speaks.

"I'm sorry," she says quietly. "He didn't make it."

I swallow hard, the words hitting like a punch to the gut. Churchill. Despite his sometimes grumpy nature, in the end the bastard always had my back. Always had some smart remarks, or some stupid jokes. His heart was always in the right place in the end. And now... he's gone. Just like that.

I clench my jaw, looking away. My fists tighten against the sheets, but it doesn't matter. Anger and grief, it isn't going to bring him back.

Langford sits on the chair beside the bed. "I know this isn't what you want to hear, but you need to rest. You lost a lot of blood. The doctors—"

"Screw the doctors." My voice comes out rough, but I don't care. "Is that thing still out there?"

Her expression hardens. "Yes but we're looking for it. But right now, you need to focus on getting better."

I don't reply. I just stare at the ceiling, my chest rising and falling with slow, measured breaths. Churchill is dead. And that bear, whatever the hell it actually is, is still out there.

"We're going to need to take some statements soon. Someone is here to see you, once you've seen them and feel comfortable answering them just let us know." Langford turns and leaves the room, carefully shutting the door behind her.

I am staring at the ceiling again, debating whether we should have answered the call. Should I have told Churchill to stay in the pub? Persuaded him to leave it as it's out of hours? Who am I kidding? We were always turning up to that call, it's our job, even when it's outside of working hours.

I hear the door start to creak open. Soft footsteps enter the room, careful but quick. Then, the chair beside my bed scrapes against the floor as someone sits down. I don't even have to look to know who it was.

"Don't you dare pretend you're asleep," Latisha says, her voice tight.

I sigh, turning my head to face her. She looks tired, her dark curls are pulled back into a messy bun, worry lines crease her forehead. Her eyes, usually sharp and full of fire, are rimmed with exhaustion. She's been crying, it's obvious.

"You're really in here again," she mutters, shaking her head. "Jesus, Marlon."

I let out a breath. "Yeah. Looks that way."

Her jaw clenches. "You almost died."

"I didn't."

"Gordon did."

That hits harder than I expected. I feel the words like a punch to the ribs, making my fresh stitches ache. I swallow, looking away.

Latisha exhales sharply, leaning forward, her elbows on her knees. "Marlon, this isn't normal. This isn't just 'the job' anymore. Whatever that thing was, it wasn't some thug with a knife. You're fighting things that shouldn't exist."

I sit up, ignoring the burning pain in my side. "You think I don't know that?" My voice comes out sharper than I mean it to. "You think I don't know what's happening out there? The city's changing, Latisha. It's not just gangs and crime anymore, it's something else. People disappearing, bodies turning up torn to pieces, and no one's got answers. Churchill deserved better than to die not knowing what he was up against."

Her lips press into a thin line. "So that's what this is?

113

Revenge?"

"No." I shake my head. "It's about doing my job. About protecting people."

Her eyes darken. "That's bullshit, Marlon. You don't even know what you're fighting! You're out there playing the hero, but you don't have a clue what's really going on."

I open my mouth to argue, but the words are stuck. Because she is right. I don't know. Not really. I have pieces. A giant bear twice the size of any grizzly bear in a country where there aren't any bears, bodies turning up ripped apart, people vanishing without a trace. But I can't see the bigger picture. Can't connect the dots. And it is driving me mad.

"I have to try," I say finally. "Because if I don't, who will?"

Latisha leans back, arms crossed tight over her chest. "You're gonna end up like Dad."

That stops me cold. I stare at her, heartbeat thudding in my ears. "What?"

"You heard me." Her voice wavers, but she holds her ground. "You're so caught up in duty, in fixing things, in proving yourself, you're gonna end up just like him."

My fingers curl into the bed sheets again. She doesn't talk about Dad. None of us do. I look away, jaw tight. "I'm not him."

"Aren't you?" She gestures at me. "Lying in a hospital bed, torn up, barely hanging on? How many more times, Marlon? How many more before I get a call saying you didn't make it?"

I have no answer for that. Silence hangs between us, heavy and unshakable.

After a long moment, she sighs. "Please. Just quit. Get out while you still can."

I shake my head. "I can't."

114

She lets out a frustrated laugh, rubbing her temples. "Why? Why the hell not?"

"Because the city isn't safe anymore," I say, voice low. "People are dying. Churchill is dead. If I walk away now, what does that mean for him? That his death was for nothing?"

She stares at me, something breaking in her eyes. "You don't owe him your life," she whispers.

I swallow. "Maybe not. But I owe him the truth. I need to know what's happening. I need to stop it."

Latisha runs a hand down her face, then stands up abruptly. "I can't watch you do this to yourself." She grabs her bag, shaking her head. "If you won't save yourself, Marlon, then I can't do it for you."

I'm not going to try to stop her. The door clicks shut behind her, leaving me alone in the silence.

My phone starts to vibrate, snapping me back from a brief moment of thought. It's Dante, my younger brother. I swipe right to answer, the phone trembling slightly in my hand. "Yeah?"

"Marlon? It's Dante." His voice comes through, a mix of concern and confusion. "What the hell happened, man? Latisha just told me you're in the hospital. What the hell are you doing there?"

I let out a breath, feeling the sharp pain in my side as I shift in the bed. "It's... bad, Dante. Something... something out there is killing people. My partner, Churchill, didn't make it either."

The silence on the other end stretches, and I can practically feel the shock hitting him. "What? Churchill's dead? Marlon, that's... damn it, that's... what happened?"

"Something that shouldn't exist. A bear. No, not a bear. Something bigger. Stronger. It—" I stop myself, frustrated by the way it sounds. "It's not just some wild animal, Dante.

115

There's something going on out there, something... unnatural."

"Unnatural?" He scoffs, though I can tell he's just trying to process. "You mean like, what? What the hell does that even mean, Marlon? You really expect me to believe this? What the hell's going on?"

I run a hand over my face, feeling the stubble there, a sign of how long I've been out of it. "I know it sounds insane. Believe me, I'm not even sure I believe it. But it's happening. People are dying, disappearing. And I'm not walking away from it."

"Damn it, Marlon," Dante mutters. "You're in the hospital because of whatever this is. And you're telling me you're not even thinking of stopping? You can't keep doing this to yourself. I need you here, man. I can't—" His voice cracks just a little, and it hits me harder than I expect. "I can't lose you, too."

"Churchill's dead, Dante," I say, my voice rougher than I want it to be. "Churchill's dead. This thing is out there, and I can't just let it keep killing people. I have to do something. I can't leave it for someone else to deal with."

"Who else is gonna deal with it, huh? What do you think this is, some mission you've gotta finish?" Dante sounds more desperate now, like he's afraid I'm slipping too far away. "You're not invincible, Marlon. You don't have to fix everything. You have to stay alive."

I close my eyes. I know he's right. I know what I'm doing isn't safe. But I can't stop. Not now. "I don't know how to stop. I need to know what this is. I need to make sure this doesn't keep happening to other people."

There's another pause, but this one feels different, like Dante's trying to understand, but he's scared for me. "You're not the only one who can find answers, you know. You've got me, you've got people who care about you. You're not alone in this, Marlon. But if you don't make it out of this, what does it all matter?"

I feel a lump forming in my throat. He's right, nothing matters if I don't make it. But walking away feels like I'm abandoning everything. "I can't just... turn my back, Dante. Not when people are depending on me."

"You've already lost too much, man. Don't make it worse." His voice cracks again, quieter this time. "I don't know how to say this, but... don't make the same mistake Dad made. Don't disappear into this like he did."

The mention of Dad again feels like a punch to the gut, and I bite back a bitter laugh. "I'm not him."

"You sure? Because it feels like it, Marlon. Lying here, torn up, because you think you have to save everyone else, but you're not thinking about yourself. I can't lose you like this."

I take a shaky breath, my chest tightening. I know what he means. I know he's scared. Hell, I'm scared too. But I can't turn away now. I can't let whatever's out there just win.

"I'm not gonna die, Dante. I won't let that happen."

"Just promise me you'll think this through. Think about the people who care about you. Please, don't make it worse." His voice softens, the edge gone. "I'll be here for you, man. Whenever you need me."

I let the silence sit for a moment, then finally speak, the words feeling heavier than they should. "I will. I promise."

And with that, I hang up, staring at the phone in my hand, wishing it were easier to walk away from this. But I know I won't. I lean back, staring at the ceiling once more. I'm not sure if I'm making the right choice, but I know I can't stop now.

NINETEEN
Duncan

The late morning air is crisp, carrying the lingering chill of early spring, but today feels surprisingly bright. Sunlight cuts through the Hearthwick streets, gleaming off the rain-damp pavement. It's the kind of morning that tries to trick you into believing winter has finally let gone, though I knew better.

It's been a few days since I last spoke to the police, since then I feel I've made some good progress. Suspicious activity regarding a company called Chimera Solutions and a possible ex-member of staff that could be hacking in and looking into files and emails regarding Duncan. I have to get more evidence, to confirm my suspicion.

Tony's Pizzas isn't supposed to open for another hour, but I push through the door anyway. The familiar bell from above the door jingles, cutting through the quiet. Inside, the place is still waking up. Chairs are stacked on tables, counters are wiped clean, and the ovens not yet fired up. The usual warmth from the kitchen is missing, replaced by the smell of cleaning solution and yesterday's lingering flour.

Behind the counter, Antonio looks up from counting the till. His expression shifts from confusion to concern when he sees me.

"You're early, we don't open for another hour." he

mutters.

"So are you." I lean against the counter. "I've been digging into Kade and Sophia's disappearance."

Antonio stiffens. His knuckles go white against the cash drawer. "You found something?"

"A name." I meet his eyes. "Chimera Solutions. Ever heard of it?"

Antonio frowns. "No. What do they do?"

"That's what I'm trying to figure out. They deal with genetic research, animal DNA, testing and stuff like that." I lower my voice. "Kade had reached out to them before he went missing, if she's reached out to them it could be the tangible piece of evidence we're looking for. Could there be something on her laptop?"

Antonio hesitates, then gives me a slow nod. "We can have a look. It's in the back."

He leads me through the quiet kitchen, past bags of flour that are stacked near the ovens. I have to weave through stacks of empty pizza boxes and trays of proofing dough. The place has a lived-in chaos, the kind only a real family-run business could have.

The back office is cramped, barely big enough for the desk, a filing cabinet and an old plastic chair. The desk is covered in scattered invoices and old menus. In the middle of it all sits Sophia's laptop. Silver, well-used, and, for the moment, our best shot at finding out where her and Kade have gone.

"She was always on that thing," Antonio says, folding his arms. "If she was talking to these people, it'll be in there."

I nod and sit down, the chair creaking as I get on. I crack my knuckle before flipping the screen open. The screen lights up, the cursor blinking like it is waiting for me to crack a code.

The first stop is her email. I type *'Chimera Solutions'*

into the search bar but nothing appears. I try a few other variations like *'Chimera'* and *'CS'* but still nothing.

I exhale, rubbing the bridge of my nose. She's found them somehow, but not through email. Maybe a deleted message? A phone call?

I'm about to move on when a soft ding echoes from the screen. A pop-up notification appears at the bottom of the screen. It reads *'Calendar Alert: CS First Assessment.'* I click on it. The event was set for a few days before she vanished. No details. No location. Just those three words.

I frown. "Antonio."

He steps closer, curious to what I've found. "What is it?"

I point at the screen. "You recognize this?"

He shakes his head. "Never seen it before."

"CS... could stand for Chimera Solutions." I exhale. "Whatever this was, it happened right before she disappeared."

Antonio rubs his jaw. "That's bad, isn't it?"

I don't answer. I click over to her browser history. A mix of cooking tutorials, grocery orders, and... There. A visit to *'www.chimerasolutions.co.uk'*. I click the link, only to be treated with: ***'404 ERROR. PAGE NOT FOUND.'***

Damn. Antonio leans over my shoulder asking "That normal?"

"No," I mutter. "Means someone shut it down. Or someone doesn't want people looking into them at the moment."

Antonio swears under his breath. "So what now?"

I close the laptop. "Now, I'm going to take this to the police. Sophia and Kade both had clues leading to this company before they disappeared, this can't be a coincidence."

He frowns, looking a bit puzzled as he does so. "You really think they'll help?"

I stand up. "PC Churchill and PC Tredon will. They're the cops I've spoken to already about this. They seem to be making small progress on it. Maybe this is the thing that'll push them in the right direction."

Antonio watches me for a long moment, then nods. "Be careful, Duncan. I feel like we're awakening something here. If this company is really behind the kidnappings, then it makes them dangerous."

I don't like the way he said that. I'm already nervous, I feel like I'm starting to become paranoid. What if we have awoken something. Dr. Heckingbottom said *'Some doors are locked for a reason. Don't make the mistake of forcing one open.'* I can't help but feel he knows something. All these warnings but I have to push through. I have to do it for Kade.

I step out of the shop, squinting against the bright morning sun. The street was still quiet. Maybe too quiet. Something feels off. The realisation of knowing the disappearances are connected is making me doubt everything.

My fingers tremble a bit as I pull out my phone and call Mum. She answers almost immediately.

"Duncan?" she says, voice tight. "Everything okay?"

"Yeah, I'm alright," I say, glancing over my shoulder. "I just spoke to Antonio. We found out Sophia was in contact with Chimera Solutions. That was a few days before she disappeared."

There's a long pause on the other end. I hear her exhale, shaky. "I'm glad you're telling me things again," she says quietly. "I've felt so shut out these past few weeks."

"I didn't mean to," I mutter.

"I know. But Duncan..." her tone shifts, sharper now. "You didn't go to school again today."

I wince. "I just needed to follow this lead. It could mean something."

"You're sixteen," she says, voice rising. "You shouldn't be investigating disappearances. That's not your job. Let the police do their work."

"But what if they're not asking the right people?" I push. "What if no one's looking in the places they should?"

"I understand why you're doing this, I do... but I'm scared, Duncan," she says, quieter now. "I can't lose you too."

The words sit heavy between us. I nod, even though she can't see it.

"I'll head home soon," I say.

"Promise me you'll at least go in tomorrow?"

"...I'll try."

She lets out a soft sigh. "Okay. Just... be careful."

"Yeah. Love you."

"Love you too."

I end the call and slip the phone back into my pocket, standing still for a second as the cold Hearthwick air bites at my face. Then I turn, shoulders tight, and start walking.

The police station is around twenty minutes by foot, fifteen at a good pace. I scan the nearby environment before turning to walk towards the high street. Nothing but a few birds flying.

I'm just setting off when something catches the corner of my eye. I turn quickly to look. A flicker of something shifts behind a distant building on the far side of the square. A shadow darting out of sight. Too fast.

My pulse kicks up. Was someone watching me? Or am I just being paranoid? I turn sharply, scanning the street again, but whoever it was has already melted away. Well, there's no time to stick around now. I take off, sprinting towards the police station. I'm taking no risks. I don't care if that was real or if I'm seeing things but I'm not staying around to find out.

Whatever I have just found whilst digging around, it

122

must be big. And if I'm being watched… that means I'm getting too close.

TWENTY
Duncan

More Mysterious Animal Attacks Leave Town on Edge:
Is the 'Beast of Black Water' to Blame Again?
- **News headline from the Daily Mail — Thursday, 17th April 2025**

I reach the police station faster than I should have, my pulse is racing from my run and the feeling of being watched outside Tony's Pizzas. The station looms ahead, its dull brick exterior as unremarkable as ever, but something feels... off.

The usual morning bustle is missing. I know the place is usually dull but not this dull. No officers chatting outside, no civilians pacing around the lobby, waiting to report some minor crime. The air feels heavy, like a storm has just passed but left destruction in its wake.

I push through the front doors and into the reception. The receptionist sees me but looks straight back down, avoiding eye contact. "I'm here to see PC Churchill and PC Tredon."

The woman doesn't reply with words, she simply shakes her head slightly whilst still looking down.

She's giving me nothing, so I head down the corridor to the right of the desk. I remember seeing some offices when I was heading to the interrogation room previously.

As I walk into the office my eyes start immediately scanning the room for PC Churchill and PC Tredon. I need to speak to them. I have a lead, one that could finally tell me what happened to my best friend.

I can't help but notice the silence. A few officers are scattered around, but no one is speaking. The officers at their desks aren't working, they are just... sitting there. A couple of them stare at their computers, hands hovering over the keys but not typing. One officer wipes his eyes before muttering something to his partner.

This isn't just low morale. It's grief. A sinking feeling settles in my stomach.

I need to talk to PC Churchill and PC Tredon. I have a lead on Kade's disappearance, something real, something they can chase. As I search for them, my gaze lands on the far side of the office, where PC Tredon sits at his desk.

My stomach drops. Tredon looks like hell. His white police shirt is rumpled and slightly stained red in parts, as if blood has soaked through. His face is long and drawn. His left arm is wrapped in a thick bandage, blood seeping through in dark patches. Scratches and deep bruises cover the side of his face, disappearing beneath the collar of his shirt. His right hand trembles slightly as he flips through stacks of paperwork, his desk looks like an absolute wreck.

I walked up to him slowly. "PC Tredon."

He turns, eyes dull, like he hasn't slept. They're bloodshot, looking hollow. When he sees me, he tries to straighten up slightly, but it doesn't do much to hide the weight pressing down on him.

"Duncan." His voice is hoarse. "Not a good time."

I ignore the warning. "I need to talk to you and Churchill. It's about Kade. I think I've got something."

His face twitches, and for the first time, I notice the way his hands are clenched at his sides, like he is barely keeping himself together.

"You didn't hear," he says, his voice barely above a whisper.

A cold weight drops in my chest. "Hear what?"

Tredon swallows hard, glancing toward the far side of the station where a desk sits empty. The desk that I assume is Churchill's.

PC Tredon inhales sharply, but his voice comes out shaky. "Late yesterday. We were out responding to a call. Some kind of disturbance at the edge of town." His jaw tightens. "Bear attack."

I stared at him. "A bear attack? We don't have bears in this county."

He nods. "That's what it was. But—" He looks away, shaking his head like he can't even get the words out. "It doesn't make sense."

I feel a strange pressure building in my chest, like my ribs have suddenly shrunk two sizes too small. Churchill had been one of the good ones in the end. He actually seemed like the kind of officer who actually gave a damn when it mattered, turns out he listened and wanted to make things better. And now, just like that, he is gone.

Tredon's hands curl into fists. "He was torn up. Badly." His voice is tight. "I should have been out there with him, not hiding away. We were meant to work together, but he wanted to be the hero." He wipes away a tear. "I should have been there."

I didn't know what to say. A heavy silence stretches between us before I finally force myself to speak. "Tredon, I'm sorry."

He just nods, still staring at the floor.

I hesitate, but I can't just walk away. "Look, I know

126

this is the worst possible time, but Kade—" I swallowed. "I've been following a lead. Chimera Solutions. I think Sophia might've been involved with them right before she disappeared, and if she was, there's a chance they were involved with Kade too."

Tredon exhales again, rubbing a hand down his face. He looks exhausted, but he gives me a slight nod. "We'll talk. Just... give me a minute. Head to the room we interviewed you in before."

I nod and step back, heading to the room. The station feels heavier than when I first walked in. Churchill is gone, and the hole he's left behind is impossible to ignore. But something is telling me that his death isn't an accident. Maybe Chimera Solutions has something to do with it, the DNA reports I stole linked Kade to the attack at Black Water Farm, and if that is the same kind of attack as downtown then who knows what's going on. Either way, I'm going to find out.

I sit down in the room on the metal chair, its feet dragging the floor as I scoot it into position. There's nothing on the table this time, last time I was here paperwork was covering it.

I hear the door creak open and see Tredon walking in cautiously. He is carrying a folder with him, documents are spewing out the side.

"Alright, what have you got?" Tredon says, placing himself on the office chair on the other side of the table.

"I went through Kade's stuff. Emails, files, you name it. There was a place he'd emailed. They're called Chimera Solutions. They specialise in animal genetics, DNA and all that kind of stuff."

Tredon coughs "And why was Kade in contact with them?"

I gather my thoughts "I don't know, but I went there. I

127

spoke to the Head of the company. He was some high tech smart-ass. He told me if some doors are closed then it's best to leave them that way, or something like that. I can't remember the exact words he used but it seemed like he didn't want me digging."

"Why would they not want you digging? Maybe they've got something to hide?" says Tredon.

"That's not the only thing." I butt in. "I overheard some of the staff talking about a hack. Someone is getting into emails and files."

"But how is that relevant?" Tredon asks.

"One of the names they mentioned was the same guy I'd come across when searching on the internet. Dr. Magnus Blackthorne. He was involved in some sort of court case a while back. Illegal animal testing or something."

Marlon looks up, as if a bright thought has just crossed his mind "The bear wasn't normal. Maybe it was some sort of hybrid, lab-born thing. This could be something related to the attacks aswell."

"Who knows but Sophia had a note on her computer about this company aswell, this can't be a coincidence." I can start to feel some adrenaline kicking in. It feels like after all the digging we're finally getting somewhere.

"Leave this with me, I'm going to see if I can conduct some interviews with this company. Maybe it'll shed some light on the whole thing, thank you Duncan."

I get up and start to head out the station. Plans are finally in action, but I'm not just going to sit here and wait, I'm going to keep digging.

TWENTY-ONE
Marlon

I'm standing outside DC Emily Langford's office, my ribs aching with every breath. The knock on her door feels like an afterthought, I'm not waiting for an invitation. Pushing inside, I find her at her desk, eyes flicking up from a screen, her expression cool and unreadable.

The office is tidy and professional. Files are organised and arranged into folders that fill shelves on the wall, a complete contrast to my workspace. DC Langford has been tasked with overseeing this investigation now. I don't know why but I feel like it should have been me that's on this.

"Morning Langford" I say, trying to force a smile through the pain.

"Marlon?" she replies, setting her pen down. "You should be home."

I ignore what she says. The air in her office feels thick, suffocating. Maybe it's just me. Maybe it was yesterday, the blood, the screams, Churchill being ripped apart before I could do a damn thing. The bear had been relentless. Unnatural.

"I want in on the investigation," I say, my voice rougher than I intend it to be. My throat is still raw from inhaling dirt and blood. "Churchill didn't deserve to die like that."

Emily exhales, her lips pressing into a thin line. "The

129

department's handling it. You need to rest."

"Look, I know they've assigned you to the case regarding the attacks, but I want to help." I sigh, swallowing before saying "Churchill was killed, his death can't be for nothing, I wanna find this thing and kill it. I've got some leads, I need you to do some digging on a company for me. They're called Chimera Solutions. I can't help but feel they're connected to these attacks."

Her eyes widen before she schools her expression. I've been a cop long enough to recognize that. Shock. Fear. A secret getting a little too close to the surface. She knows something.

She leans forward, elbows on her desk. "Marlon," she says, her voice softer now, almost pleading. "You need to go home. Rest. You're in no shape for this."

I let out a humorless laugh. "I'm fine."

"It sounds like you're losing it. This Chimera place, how is it connected?"

"It's just a hunch at the moment, they deal with animal DNA research—"

Langford cuts me out before I can finish. "And that makes them send fifteen foot savage bears into the street of Hearthwick? Listen to yourself Tredon... I know you lost Churchill, and I know he was your friend, but you can't just go on a wild goose chase, gunning for whoever you've got a feeling is to blame."

"Look, I'm not losing it, I swear." Sweat drips down my face, stinging against my graze.

"Marlon, go home." Her jaw clenches. "This conversation is over."

I scoff, stepping back. "Right."

The second I turn, my boss is already striding towards me, like he's been waiting for this moment.

"Tredon," DCI Hewitt barks. "My office. Now."

I follow him, dragging my feet, already knowing where this is heading. Hewitt shuts the door behind us and fixes me with that look of his, the one that makes rookies sweat.

"You're off duty," he says. "Effective immediately. You need time to recover."

"I'm fine." I snap back.

"You're not," he shoots back, his voice edged with frustration. "Jesus, Marlon, you almost died. And Churchill—" He stops himself, running a hand over his face. "Go home. Get some rest."

I set my jaw. "And if I don't?"

"Then I'll make it official."

I stare at him, heartbeat hammering. There is no fighting this. I turn and leave before he can say anything else.

Back at my desk, I scour over the files arrayed over it, I'm going to bring some of them with me. I grab some of the forensic and witness reports, shoving them into my bag while no one's looking. I need to bring whatever I can, if I can't find this thing while at work, I'll find it outside.

As I turn to leave, I catch Langford watching me from her office, her expression unreadable. Suspicion coils in my gut. Something is off with her.

131

TWENTY-TWO
Duncan

I really miss Kade. I'm confident he'll be all okay when we find him. Actually, no. I'm not. I'm scared. Every day that passes and he's not here I lose more and more hope. I have no idea where he is and that scares me.

- ***Diary entry from Duncan Webb — Saturday, 19th April 2025***

I stare at the evidence board I put together yesterday, it's a mess. Red string's connecting blurry photos, handwritten notes, and printouts from sketchy forums. At the center of it all are two names: Chimera Solutions and Dr. Magnus Blackthorne.

Kade had vanished without a trace, and every lead I've chased so far had led me down a rabbit hole, not knowing if what I'm digging up is relevant or even real... until now. Blackthorne wasn't just some obscure scientist. His name has cropped up in a handful of classified reports, tied to experiments that sounded more like science fiction than reality. If anyone had the means to make someone disappear, it was him.

It's been two days since I spoke to PC Tredon and I'm yet to hear back from him. I've let Aaron and his friend Joe in on the investigation now. I haven't told them all the information that I've found yet, but I have said to them that I've got some leads. They were the ones that were supposed to meet Kade on the day he disappeared and are good friends with him. Even though I've not spent too much time with them in the past they seemed really up for it yesterday when I called them.

I feel like my team will work well, surely it's got to work better with more eyes looking for leads. Aaron is very good with computers so having someone that's going to be good at digging could be a game changer. Joe on the other hand... he's just Joe. He isn't the most tech-savvy or tactical thinker. He tends to go down the rabbit-hole of conspiracy theories and make-believe.

I grab my phone and call Aaron.

"Yeah?" His voice comes through, slightly muffled, probably because he was halfway through a snack or typing something ridiculously fast like usual.

"I need your help," I say, trying to sound more confident than I feel. "It's about Kade. It's time I fill you in on what I've got. Meet me at Joe's?"

I grab my pre-packed bag and head out the front door. I'm bringing as much paperwork as I can cram in beside my laptop. There are a few packets of biscuits on the coffee table in the living room, so I grab them aswell as I am passing through the house.

I'm halfway out the door, hoodie on and backpack slung over one shoulder, when Mum's voice cuts through from the kitchen.

"Duncan?"

I freeze. "Yeah?"

She steps into the hallway, drying her hands on a tea towel, eyes narrowing just slightly. "Where are you going? It's nearly dark."

"I'm heading to Joe's," I say, trying to sound casual. "Him and Aaron want to help me look into the disappearances. Just... research stuff."

Her brows knit together for a second, but then she nods slowly. "Alright. As long as you're safe. No sneaking off into woods or abandoned buildings, okay?"

"We're not doing anything stupid," I promise. "Just internet stuff, digging through old forums and articles."

She sighs but offers a small smile. "Okay. Just check in with me later, yeah?"

"Yeah, I will."

I give her a quick nod and slip out the door before she can change her mind. Luckily for me Joe's house is only around fifteen minutes away so I don't need a lift. My bike is lying in the garage, waiting to be used, so I take it. By the time I cycle there, Aaron and Joe are already waiting for me outside the house.

Joe's house sits in the middle of a quiet street, the kind of place where nothing ever seems to happen. The outside is neat. His parents keep the lawn trimmed and the hedges perfect, but the inside has that comfortably messy, lived-in feel. The moment I step through the front door, I can hear the low hum of a football game playing from the living room. The scent of something fried lingers in the air, making my stomach growl.

Joe's dad, a broad-shouldered man with a perpetual five o'clock shadow, glances up from the sofa as we walk in. "You boys staying for dinner?" he asks, his voice gruff but not unkind.

"Not tonight, Dad," Joe calls back. "Just heading to the basement."

His dad grunts, his attention already drifting back to the game. "Try not to burn the house down."

"No promises," Joe mutters under his breath, leading us past the kitchen and down the narrow staircase.

"So, this is where the magic happens" Joe gloats, spreading his arms to show the room.

The basement has been set up by Joe by the look of it. Our new unofficial HQ. A mix of old furniture, mismatched chairs, and a beaten-up couch surrounds the far side of the room. Posters of old bands and action movies cover the walls, some of them peeling at the edges. The place smells faintly of dust, energy drinks, and whatever forgotten snacks have been left down here too long. It isn't fancy, but it's ours.

Joe's parents didn't ask many questions when he set this up apparently, which helps. Aaron has his laptop set up, wires snaking across the old carpet, while Joe leans back in a beanbag chair, twirling a pen between his fingers.

I lay out everything I had on Chimera Solutions and Blackthorne as Joe and Aaron take it in. I can see them nodding and thinking at what I tell them.

"We were supposed to meet Kade that day," Joe mutters, shaking his head. "He never showed. We thought maybe he got held up or changed his mind. But this? You think this Blackthorne guy might have taken him?"

"I think Blackthorne could be involved, one way or another," I reply. "He's my main suspect, I just need proof."

Aaron adjusts his glasses and cracks his knuckles. "Give me a few hours. If there's anything digital on this guy, I'll find it."

Time crawls by as Aaron works. The only sounds are the rapid clicking of his keyboard and the occasional rustle of a snack wrapper. Joe scrolls through his phone, probably reading conspiracy theories again. I can't help but pace around the room. I was getting better at keeping my nerves in check, but waiting like this still makes my stomach twist.

GONE BEFORE THE MOON

"Blackthorne's name isn't popping up in the usual places," Aaron mutters. "But... wait. Hang on." His fingers fly across the keyboard. "This is weird. Looks like he had some funding cut off a few years back when he was working for Chimera. Some of his projects went dark after that. Seems like someone scrubbed most of his records after that, but I can still see traces here and there."

Joe yawns. "Maybe the government is trying to cover it up."

"Why would the government cover it up? It seems like someone is erasing all details of him off the internet. It could be anyone. Seems to be black holes of information in places, stuff definitely missing. And... wait a second—"

Joe and I sit up. "What?" we both say at the same time.

Aaron's lips curl into a grin. "He made an unusual purchase last year. An old, abandoned storage facility on the outskirts of town. Paid in cash through shell companies, but it all kind of traces back to him. Like some of the information is deleted but it's pointing in his direction."

I frown. "A storage facility? That's not exactly a high-tech lab. Why would he want that?"

Aaron glances at me. "That's what we're gonna find out."

Joe lets out a low whistle. "This is starting to feel like a horror movie."

"Hopefully one where we don't get killed in the first act," I mutter. "So, what's our plan?"

Aaron keeps digging. "Wait, there's more... some strange activity near that facility. Unregistered deliveries, unusual power usage. Something's happening there. Whoever is trying to cover this up is doing a good job. To get most of the information removed is like high tech stuff. I'm literally picking up breadcrumbs here, but I think I've got it right."

Joe taps his foot anxiously. "Think it's just a front?"

"Either that, or it's a lab off the grid," Aaron says. "Either way, it's worth checking out."

"How far away is it?" I ask.

Aaron scratches his chin, "About five miles. It's a bit outside the city but it's towards Eldermere."

"That's where Chimera is" My hands sweat and I start to feel shaky. "Let's go pay this place a visit tomorrow. See what it's all about."

I stand up to stretch my legs, the cramp begins to fade. "I'm gonna give PC Tredon a ring, let him know what we're doing. He seems like he's one of the good ones."

"Sounds good," replies Joe.

I pull out my phone and dial PC Tredon's number, but it goes straight to voicemail. "Hey PC Tredon, just wanted to give you an update about our findings. We think we've found somewhere that Dr. Blackthorne might be hiding, we're gonna check it out tomorrow."

Outside, the quiet suburban streets stretch into the night, streetlights flickering. This is way bigger than just finding Kade now. Whatever Blackthorne is up to, it isn't good. And we are walking straight into it.

TWENTY-THREE
Marlon

I sit in the dim glow of my laptop screen, the only light in my flat aside from the occasional flicker of a streetlamp outside. My eyes burn, my head pounding, but I can't stop. Sleep has become an afterthought these past few days, something other people did. Not me. Not while Churchill is dead and the thing that killed him is still out there. A bear. In England. It makes no sense.

I scratch the stubble that's grown on my face, my fingers start to hover over the keyboard as I force myself to relive it again. The butcher shop, the radio static, the way Gordon's pleas had turned into a scream so fast my brain hadn't caught up. The sheer size of it, bigger than any animal I've ever seen. Muscles rippling beneath thick fur. I see the blood again, and hear the crack of bone. I remember my own breath, fast and uneven, the clever shaking in my grip as I held it. The bear hardly flinched. It should've gone down. It should've died. Instead, it tore Gordon apart and left me with nothing but nightmares and questions.

I rub my face, trying to force the memory back where it belongs. I've been through every official report, scoured every wildlife record I can access. Nothing. No sightings, no zoo escapes, no imports gone wrong. Nothing that can explain how a goddamn bear, one big enough to rip a man apart, had

138

been roaming the city.

I sip what is left of my cold coffee, clicking through yet another forum post about cryptid sightings. This is the desperate part. The part I won't even admit to myself. I'm a cop, not some conspiracy theorist, chasing legends. But when reality stops making sense, you start looking in places you normally wouldn't.

I look up at the search bar. "What sort of bear could even do that?" I murmur under my breath.

'The biggest bear species in the world is the polar bear, standing at nearly ten feet tall on their hind legs.' The first google answer isn't helpful. I'm no animal scientist but this bear was far bigger than that, and it wasn't white.

I keep searching. That's when I find it, a grainy photo, buried in the depths of an old discussion thread. It shows a hulking shape, deep in the woods, barely visible through the blur and pixelation. The posts author claims they had seen an Arctotherium.

I have to look it up, I have no idea what it is. Turns out it's a South American short-faced bear. It's been extinct for thousands of years. And yet here it is, in a photo taken less than a year ago, attached to some half-baked blog post about prehistoric survivors.

Looking at the comments, most people dismissed it as a hoax. I might have too, if I hadn't already seen the impossible with my own eyes.

I scroll further down the page, to the bottom of the post. *'Photo by: Richard Lanesworth.'*

I copy the name and start searching. It doesn't take me long to find an old social media profile. A few more clicks and I have an address. It's somewhere fancy, out in the countryside, not far from the last confirmed sighting of my bear.

A knock on the door makes me jump. My breath

catches in my throat as I turn towards it. "Open up, Marlon."

It's Latisha. I exhale sharply and run a hand through my unkempt hair before unlocking the door. She steps inside, her eyes immediately scanning the mess I've made of my flat.

"Jesus," she mutters. "You look like hell."

"Nice to see you too," I reply, shutting the door.

She folds her arms. "How long's it been since you slept?"

I glance at the laptop screen. "Few hours here and there."

She gives me a look that could burn a hole through my skull. "That's a lie."

I sigh, pinching the bridge of my nose. "I'm onto something, Tish."

"You need to rest."

"I can't."

Her jaw tightens. "You can't bring Churchill back, Marlon."

"That's not what this is."

"Then what is it?" she snaps. "Because from where I'm standing, it looks like you're spiraling. Obsessing over something that no one else even thinks is real."

I open my mouth to argue, but she isn't done. "You think you're the only one who lost someone? You think I want to watch you go down with this?"

I clench my fists. "This isn't about me."

She scoffs. "No? Then why the hell do you look like a ghost? Why can't you even function like a normal person?"

"Because I can't stop seeing it. Can't stop hearing it." I plead. "It's out there Tish, it has to be stopped."

She shakes her head. "I can't watch you do this to yourself."

She turns and leaves before I can say anything else.

140

The door clicks shut, leaving me alone with the hum of my laptop and the pounding in my skull.

I sigh and rub my temples, but something outside catches my eye. A car. Black. Parked on the opposite side of the street to where Tish's car was. Was it there before?

I stand slowly, moving towards the window. I can't make out the driver. The engine is off. The car just sits there. I swallow hard, my pulse quickening. Am I being watched? Have I already dug too deep? How would anybody know?

Minutes pass, and then, without warning, the car starts up and pulls away, disappearing down the road. I let out a breath I didn't realise I was holding. Paranoia. That's all it is. I am exhausted, working myself into a frenzy. Right?

I shake it off and walk back to my laptop. I have bigger things to worry about right now. Lanesworth's name sticks with me. I start searching deeper, looking for any connections. That's when I find something else. Something worse. A past case. A missing hiker. Seven months ago, a young man had vanished near the same woods Lanesworth had taken the photo. His body was never found. No evidence. Just a last known location and a few frantic calls to emergency services that led nowhere. It seems the investigation is over now.

I read the report twice, my chest tightening. The case has been buried under other missing person reports, dismissed as just another unfortunate accident. But what if it wasn't? What if he had seen the bear too?

I lean back in my chair, my reflection staring back at me from the laptop screen. Dark circles under my eyes, stubble growing wild along my jaw.; I barely recognize myself. Latisha is right about one thing—I am spiraling. But she is wrong about the rest. I'm not going to stop. I grab my coat and my keys. Time to pay Mr. Lanesworth a visit.

TWENTY-FOUR
Marlon

I grip the steering wheel, eyes fixed on the winding country road ahead. My headlights carve twin beams through the thickening darkness, the surrounding fields are swallowed in blackness. My phone has no signal out here, and I haven't seen any cars for miles. The further I drive, the more I feel like I am leaving the world behind. Then, with a sputter and a lurch, my car stutters to a halt.

"Of course," I mutter, thumping the steering wheel.

I try the ignition again. Nothing. The engine is dead. I exhale sharply, running a hand down my face before glancing at the GPS. The route had frozen a few minutes ago, just before my signal cut out. I am close to Lanesworth's estate, but I'm not sure exactly how close.

I step out, my breath misting in the cold air. The night is silent except for the rustling of wind through the trees. I retrieve a flashlight from the glove compartment and click it on. A weak beam cut through the dark, barely illuminating the road ahead. There are no streetlights, just a narrow, cracked lane with thick hedgerows on either side.

I sigh and lock the car. If Lanesworth's house is nearby, I can at least reach it on foot and figure out what to do next.

I start hobling, the crunch of gravel beneath my boots the only sound accompanying me. The air smells of damp earth and old wood, the scent of the deep countryside. I can just about make out the silhouette of a wooden signpost up ahead, overgrown with ivy. I push the leaves aside and squint at the faded lettering. *'Lanesworth Manor – 1 Mile.'* One mile; Not ideal, but manageable. I adjust my coat and press forward.

The road narrows into a dirt path, bordered by towering oak trees whose branches claw at the sky. My flashlight flickers, and I smack it against my palm to keep it steady. Something rustles in the undergrowth to my left, and I freeze, ears straining. A fox darts out and scurries across the path. I exhale, shaking my head at myself before continuing.

As I walk, my mind drifts to why I am here. From my investigation, while researching Lanesworth I found that he had once been a well-connected man, someone who knew things about the city's underbelly. From his social media he has gone quiet the past year or so. That was about the time that the photo was uploaded. With his connections, I feel if anyone has answers about the disappearances and the increasing chaos, it might be him.

The trees thin, revealing a vast open field. In the distance, past a wrought-iron gate, stands a looming house. Even in the darkness, I can see the shape of it. It's tall, with turrets and sharp gables, its stone exterior seems worn by time. One window on the upper floor glows faintly, the only sign of life within.

I reach the gate and test it. Locked. I glance around before stepping to the side, finding a gap in the hedge. With a grunt, I push through, branches snagging at my coat. On the other side, I dust myself off and approach the front door. The house feels… watchful.

Taking a breath, I raise my fist and knock. The sound echoes through the still night. I wait. A floorboard creaks inside, then, the door slowly opens, about a quarter of the way before stopping on a chain.

"Who are you, what do you want?" Says a posh voice.

"My name's PC Tredon, I'm here to speak to Mr. Lanesworth."

"What do you want with me?" He sputters back, panicked. His tone is concerning. Why is he so nervous?

"There's an investigation going on at the moment, we feel like you might have some information that might be of use to us." Reaching into my pocket I pull out my police badge. "Do you mind if I come in?"

The chain unhooks from the door, setting it free. Mr. Lanesworth opens it and puts his hand out, gesturing for me to come in.

"Take a seat on one of the chairs in there. I'll make a cup of tea." Mr. Lanesworth points to the room on the right of the large staircase that cuts the entrance hall in half.

There is a large chandelier hanging in the open space of the hall, with lots of LED candle lights being held up by the feature. Paintings litter the walls, making it feel like something out of a murder mystery film.

As I walk through the large wooden door opening, I see a spacious lounge area. The lounge stretches wide and elegant. Plush, velvet-upholstered chairs and long, tufted sofas are arranged in clusters around polished mahogany coffee tables. An ornate fireplace, large enough to stand in, dominates one wall, its mantle adorned with antique candelabras and more framed portraits of what I assume are long-gone ancestors. The tall, arched windows are framed with heavy drapes overlooking the sprawling estate, their glass panes catching the flickering light from the roaring fire. The scent of aged wood, leather-bound books, and faint traces of cigar smoke linger in the air, giving the room an atmosphere of quiet power and timeless luxury.

"How many sugars do you take?" Lanesworth's voice echoes through the doorway.

"Two please, and a splash of milk."

After a few moments, Lanesworth brings me a steaming mug of tea in a fine china cup. His purple velvet dressing gown flows behind him as he walks.

"I'm sorry, but I'm more of a whisky man," he says, grabbing a bottle of Dalmore Whisky from the side.

He sits on the chair beside me and proceeds to pour a small amount into an empty glass after brushing his hands through his wavy grey hair.

I have to try and find out what he knows. Maybe I can see if he was in the area when the attack happened the other day. I take a sip of the tea before setting it down on the table.

"Mr. Lanesworth, I'm assuming you've seen the news the past couple of days. We've had reports that you were in town the night of the Bear attack. Can you confirm where you were?"

He raises an eyebrow as he swirls the whisky in his glass. "In town? I hardly go into town these days, Officer Tredon. Too much noise, too many people."

"So you weren't anywhere near the area where the attack happened?" I press.

He smirks, but there's a tightness in his expression. "Are you suggesting I had something to do with that... beast? I don't know why you think I would."

"I'm just asking routine questions," I reply evenly. "You understand why I have to be thorough. Did you see anything unusual in the days leading up to the attack? Anyone suspicious hanging around? Any strange deliveries to your property?"

He exhales sharply with an air of confusion. Probably because he doesn't get why I would think he'd have anything to do with the bear. "Nothing out of the ordinary. I keep to myself, Officer. I enjoy my privacy."

I nod slowly, watching him closely. He's guarded. "Alright, let's talk about something else then. I'm also here about a photo that you uploaded around a year ago, the one of the bear."

"That photo was deleted, that's impossible." He gets up from his chair swiftly. "You don't want to keep digging into this. I suggest you stop there."

"Why? What's going on?" I ask, noting the shift in his demeanor. "Withholding information from the police is a crime, you know that, right?" I press.

He scratches his head and paces the room. "They told me to keep quiet. They—"

"Who's they?" I butt in.

Lanesworth shakes his head, muttering under his breath before turning back to me. "You don't understand. I made a mistake, alright? A stupid mistake. And now I have to live with it."

I lean forward, lowering my voice. "A mistake like what? Uploading a picture? What made that bear so special that someone would threaten you over it?"

His eyes dart toward the door, then back at his phone on the table. He looks like a man caught in a trap. "That was no ordinary bear," he murmurs, more to himself than to me.

"No kidding," I say. "That thing tore through the town and killed my colleague. So if you know something, you need to tell me."

He swallows, gripping his whisky glass a little too tightly. "I thought it was just some freak of nature when I took that picture. Something rare. Something fascinating." His voice lowers. "But they saw it. They came to me."

I narrow my eyes. "They? Who are 'they'?"

Lanesworth exhales sharply and rubs his forehead. "I can't say their name. It's dangerous even talking about this."

I cross my arms, unimpressed. "So you'd rather let people die? Let that thing roam free?"

He hesitates, then sits back down heavily. "It's bigger than you think, officer. Bigger than some rogue animal. It's... controlled."

My stomach tightens. "Controlled? By who?"

Lanesworth shakes his head violently. "Enough. You need to leave this alone." His hand moves toward his phone, his thumb hovering over the screen. His eyes flicker with something between fear and resolve.

My gut twists. He's calling someone. Someone who could shut this conversation down for good.

I lean in, my voice dropping to a near whisper. "Lanesworth, don't do this. If you know something that could help me stop this before more people get hurt, you need to talk."

He hesitates, his hand trembling over the phone. His lips part as if he wants to say something, but then his jaw clenches. "You don't understand what they can do. What they will do."

"Try me."

A long silence hangs between us. Then, just as I think he might crack, he presses the call button. My heart pounds as the dial tone hums through the air.

Panic surges through me. I can't let him make this call. My body moves before I can think. I lunge forward, snatching the phone from his grasp and hurling it against the wall. The device shatters, pieces scattering across the floor. But it is too late. The faint sound of ringing still carries through the room.

Lanesworth's face is twisted with fury as he shouts toward the wreckage, "Hello? Help! Someone—"

A muffled voice crackles from the damaged speaker. I freeze. I have no idea who is on the other end, but I know I can't stay here. My pulse pounds in my ears as I bolt out the room and towards the front door as fast as I can. Only a few days ago I was attacked badly, moving this quickly hurts like hell. I grip the handle of the front door and yank it. It's locked.

"Damn it." I sputter.

Through the door to the lounge I can see Lanesworth scrambling towards a cabinet. The metallic click of a revolver being loaded sends ice through my veins. I have seconds, maybe less. My body isn't moving like it used to. Every step feels like dragging dead weight. Gritting my teeth through the pain, I stagger toward a large armchair on the far side of the room. It's not fast or graceful. I practically collapse behind it, my breath ragged as I press myself into the shadows. Lanesworth begins creeping through the manor, gun in hand.

His slow, deliberate steps echo off the wooden floor. "You shouldn't have done that," he murmurs, voice taut with tension. "You have no idea what you've gotten yourself into."

Lanesworth turns to look into another room so I get up as quietly as I can and move towards one of the corridors. I barely breathe as I manoeuvre myself through the dimly lit passage, keeping low. The house is a maze of old furniture, high archways, and antique decor that cast eerie, shifting shadows. Every step has to be perfect. Then a floorboard groans beneath my weight. I suck in a sharp breath.

I hear Lanesworth turn instantly. "Where are you?" His voice cuts through the silence. His footsteps quicken, heading straight for me.

Desperation claws at my chest as I scan for an escape. Then, I see it... a window slightly ajar. I dart towards it, fumbling the latch with my shaky hands before forcing it open. Cold air rushes in. I haul myself up and through, a graze on my

148

shoulder scraping against the frame before I tumble onto the grass below.

No time to stop. I scramble to my feet and push into a limping run across the garden, leaping over hedges and crashing through flower beds. The iron fence looms ahead. With one last push, I vault over it, hitting the dirt road on the other side.

Gasping, I turn back. The window I've escaped through stands open, curtains fluttering in the night air. Lanesworth appears, his eyes searching across the garden.

I don't wait to see if he spots me. I take off down the gravel driveway, desperate to reach my car. But just as I near the front of the estate, headlights sweep across the path. A black vehicle skids to a stop. The door swings open, and out steps a massive figure.

At least seven feet tall, with arms thicker than any human should have. The mans eyes scan the manor before he charges toward it, moving with terrifying speed. I have no idea who, or what he is, but I'm not about to stick around to find out.

I turn and run into the darkness, the towering figure disappearing behind me as I flee into the night.

TWENTY-FIVE
Duncan

Red Hat,
The specimen is ready. Faster, stronger, and more resilient than any human should be. The conditioning holds—for now. But instincts are harder to erase. Handle with care.
Payment first. No exceptions.
You know where to find me. Don't be late.
—Dr Magnus Blackthorne
- ***Letter from Dr Magnus Blackthorne to "Red Hat" — Sunday, 20th April 2025***

"Yo Duncan, wake up!" Joe's voice trails across the basement to where I'm lying, folded and awkward on the sofa.

"Jesus man, what time is it?" my eyes struggle to adjust to the light of the room. "Shit! I didn't set an alarm."

Aaron stretches his arms out yawning "It's nearly ten o'clock, let's get ready so we can head out."

I grab my backpack that lies next to the sofa and open it. I toss out the remaining paperwork that is left in there and stuff my hoodie in. The papers flutter onto the floor. There's a chocolate bar and a banana on the old wooden coffee table next to me so I grab them, stuffing them past the hoodie and into the bottom of my bag.

"Alright let's go." Joe says, waiting by the door to leave.

The ride from Joe's house to the warehouse is smooth at first, the three of us are pedaling hard under the mid-morning sun. The streets are mostly empty, just a few cars rolling past, their drivers oblivious to what we are up to. As we leave the main roads behind, the air smells of old concrete, the kind of scent that clings to forgotten places.

The further we ride, the worse the path gets. Cracked asphalt turns into dirt, then into something that barely resembles a trail. Weeds sprout out in thick clumps, roots sticking out like nature's version of spike traps. I have to swerve more than once to avoid wiping out. Joe, up ahead, is handling it like it is nothing, while Aaron is barely dodging the worst of it.

Then, just as I start to think we might make it all the way to the warehouse on our bikes, the path disappears under a mess of vines and brambles. There is no way we are riding through it.

"This is it," Joe says, hopping off his bike and dragging it towards some nearby bushes.

Aaron sighs. "Guess we're walking from here."

I follow their lead, hiding my bike in the undergrowth before stepping into the trees. The overgrown woodland swallows us quickly, the sunlight barely making it through the thick canopy above. Every step is a struggle. Twigs are snapping under our feet, low-hanging branches smack at my arms, and the ground is uneven, littered with rocks and fallen logs. The deeper we go, the heavier the air feels. It's humid, thick with the smell of moss and decay.

It feels like we are pushing through forever, but then, finally, the trees start to thin out, and we stumble into a clearing. There it is. The warehouse.

It looms ahead like a rusted skeleton. The metal walls look streaked with grime, patches of ivy creep up the sides. The place looks dead, abandoned... but also like something that has no business being left alone. A tall metal fence surrounds the entire property, chain-links are rusted but are still standing strong, with coils of barbed wire running along the top. There's no easy way in.

Joe exhales. "Well... that's a problem."

Aaron cracks his knuckles. "Nah. Just means we've got to get creative."

I swallow hard, glancing around. Whatever is waiting for us inside, we are past the point of turning back now. I peer through the chains in the fence and can see some movement on the far side of the loading dock. Someone seems to be watching something and I can't quite make out what it is.

I point to the man. "Who do you think this guy is?"

"He is acting like some kind of security, he's not dressed like one though." Joe mutters, squinting at the man.

There is a gate with a chain on it that he is guarding, but why would he be guarding this place? The building looks abandoned, surely something has to be going on here.

We all start to search the perimeter of the fence, the barbed wire and interlocking metal chains aren't giving us an inch to squeeze through. This place might be old but there seems to be no way of getting in.

"Guys look!" Aaron shouts, pointing to an overhanging tree. "This tree is high enough and overhangs most of the fence, I reckon we could get in this way."

The tree is around five meters high and hangs over most of the fence, covering over the barbed wire. There is a rusty blue storage container on the other side which is only a few feet below where the tree drapes over. This is it, this is the way in.

"I'll go first, give me a leg up" Aaron says, eyes filled with excitement at seeing a chance to show his athleticism.

I kneel down next to the tree, putting my hands together to form a step for Aaron to use. He steps on and I raise him up. He grabs onto a low branch and uses his strength to pull himself up.

"Alright Joe, your turn" I say, still in position.

We managed to lift Joe up and with the help of both Aaron and Joe they managed to pull me up to the lower branches.

Perched on a thick, gnarled branch, I wipe my sweaty palms against my jeans and glance down. The barbed wire is a good six feet below. But just beyond it, the blue storage container sits waiting, its metal surface is dented and weathered. If we can make it onto that, we're inside. No climbing, no cutting, just a clean drop.

Aaron shifts beside me, testing his footing on the branch. "Alright," he whispers. "We aim for the top of the container. Land steady, roll if you have to."

"Easy for you to say," I mutter, eyeing the gap. It isn't far, maybe a few feet, but far enough that if I screw up, I'll either hit the wire or the ground.

Joe goes first. Without hesitation, he crouches low, tenses his legs, and springs forward. He lands with a dull thud on the container's metal roof, his knees bending to absorb the impact. He straightens up and gives us a quick thumbs-up.

Aaron is next. He shuffles back slightly, then leaps. His landing is heavier than Joe's, but he sticks it, steadying himself with one hand before glancing back at me.

I swallow hard. My turn. I take a deep breath, adjust my footing, then push off. For a split second, I feel weightless, my arms flailing slightly as the container rushes towards me. My feet hit the metal, but my balance is off. I stumble, barely stopping myself from falling over the side. Joe catches my arm and yanks me upright.

"You good?" he asks.

"Yeah," I exhale, heart pounding.

Aaron is already moving, crouching near the edge of the container and peering down. "Alright, next step," he whispers. "Drop down onto the floor, then make a run to that door." He points to a silver metal door. "We can hopefully find a way inside from there."

TWENTY-SIX
Duncan

The cold metal door won't budge, no matter how hard we push. The door looks sealed to the frame, from age and neglect.

"Maybe something heavy is pressed against it" I ask, keeping my voice low.

Joe yanks at the rusted handle of the side door again, but it doesn't budge. "Locked," he mutters under his breath, stepping back.

Aaron runs his hand along the edge of the door, testing for any weak spots. "Figures," he says. "This place might be abandoned, but someone still wants to keep people out."

I glance around, my pulse quickening. The factory yard stretches out behind us, a wasteland of cracked pavement and overgrown weeds. If we make too much noise, whoever is guarding the front might hear us.

Joe takes a step back, eyeing the door like he is about to kick it in. Aaron grabs his shoulder. "Yeah, no. That's a great way to get caught."

"Then what do you suggest?" Joe shoots back.

I run my fingers over the wall, feeling the old metal siding. "What about a window?" I whisper.

Aaron nods and gestures for us to follow. We keep low, moving along the wall until we reach a set of grimy, half-broken windows just above eye level. The glass is cracked but still intact. They're streaked with dust and dirt so thick I can barely see inside.

Joe taps the glass with his knuckle. "If we break it, that guard might hear."

"Not if we do it right," Aaron replies.

He pulls off his hoodie, wrapping it around his fist, and gives the weakest pane a sharp, controlled hit. The glass cracks but doesn't shatter completely. He works at it carefully, pulling loose shards away until there is a gap big enough to reach through.

I glance around nervously. The front entrance is out of sight, but the idea of someone patrolling still makes my skin crawl. "Hurry up," I mutter.

Joe reaches in first, fumbling around until we hear the soft click of a latch. "Got it."

Aaron pushes the window open the rest of the way and gives me a look. "You first."

Of course. I sigh and grab the ledge so I can hoist myself up. The window frame is rough with rust, it's biting into my palms as I wriggle through. The moment my feet hit the ground inside, the air feels different. It's cooler, dustier, and heavy with the scent of old oil.

I turn and motion for the others. Joe slips in next, landing with barely a sound, followed by Aaron, who dusts himself off and takes a quick look around.

The room we've entered is some kind of kitchen. I'm not sure what they are making here but it looks kind of industrial. There's a massive rubbish dispenser overflowing with stinking, thrown away junk; a mix of rotten food and empty packaging. The middle of the room is split by various cabinets and cupboards. All of them look cold and metallic.

We make our way through to a door on the far side of

156

the room, being careful not to make a sound. Slowly, Aaron pushes open the door, letting out a slight creek as it becomes ajar. This door leads into the main workshop for the factory. The factory is dark, the only light is what's filtering in through cracks and broken panels in the roof. Machines stand like giants in the shadows, rusted conveyor belts frozen in time.

Aaron crouches low. "Stay quiet. We don't know who else might be in here."

I swallow hard and nod. We are in. Now comes the hard part. We make our way to a stack of boxes that are piled on a wooden pallet about five meters beyond the door, partly hiding it from the rest of the room. Peeking out from behind I spot a few people that are standing, talking.

"Who do you think they are?" Joe whispers.

"I'm not sure, let's just see what they do." I reply, squinting to look at them.

The group of people stand around in a rough circle, they are around a grimy old assembly table.

"That's Dr. Stephen Heckingbottom" I gasp. "He was the head of Chimera Solutions. I spoke to him about Kade not long ago."

"What the hell is he doing here?" asks Aaron.

"I'm not sure but I want to find out." I scurry forward, behind a different pile of boxes, these ones within earshot.

Dr. Heckingbottom stands tall, well-groomed, and dressed smartly but casually. His posture is calm and composed, like a man who already owns the world. The others, however, I have no idea who they are, but they look important and dangerous.

To Heckingbottom's right stands a man in a dark suit jacket and slacks. I recognise him aswell. Not from in person, but from my research. It's Dr. Blackthorne. What the hell is he doing with Dr. Heckingbottom? He's keeping his hands in his pockets, but there is something about the way he stands that makes me uneasy, like he is constantly calculating something. He doesn't speak much, just watching.

Just to his right, almost hiding at the edge of the group, a figure stands apart from the rest, wearing a hood that shadows most of his face. Unlike the others, he doesn't move much. He barely even breathes. There is something unsettling about him, something wrong. My gut twists, but I can't place why.

Next to him, a woman stands with her arms crossed. She is fit, with the kind of stance that screams authority, even though she isn't in any kind of uniform. Her gaze flicks over the others, sharp and assessing. A cop? A former soldier? Whoever she is, she isn't just here to watch. She looks familiar, I just can't pin where from,

"Stephen, we've been getting some suspicion on us. A cop, by the name of Marlon. He's poking his nose around too much, and thinks Chimera is linked to the bear attacks and disappearances." Her voice is authoritative yet calm.

"Wait, Langford... I've seen that guy. He showed up at my manor last night." Says a man to her right, adjusting his tie.. "We scared him off but I feel he knows too much. Stephen, what can we do?"

Langford? That's one of the officers from the police station. What's she doing here?

The guy that spoke to her is an older, posh looking thin man, wearing an expensive-looking suit. He has an air of nervousness about him, fingers twitching slightly every time he looks around. He keeps glancing at Heckingbottom, as if seeking reassurance.

"We'll deal with him, don't worry. If he's poking around thinking Chimera Solutions are behind everything, then there's a risk he finds who we actually are. I'll sort it out."

Replies Heckingbottom.

I have to warn PC Tredon, I think they're going to try and kill him. As soon as I get out of here I'm going to call him. I don't know what he meant by that. So, Chimera isn't behind everything then who is?

A voice echoes from the entrance of the factory. "Glad I could join you."

It's a man in a red top hat. He stands out immediately, not just because of the ridiculous hat, but because of the way he carries himself. It's like he owns the whole damn room. He leans lazily against the table as he gets to it, smirking, completely at ease. Something tells me he isn't the kind of guy you want to owe money to. "So, what is it that The Black Veil has got for me?" he adds, placing a metal case on the table.

Dr. Heckingbottom speaks, his voice smooth and measured. "Now that everyone is here, let's begin what this is really about. This isn't just a deal, gentlemen. This is the future. We thank you greatly for your investments, we couldn't have extended our research and developments as much as we have without you. We've done what science could only dream of. And now, for those who have the means, we offer power beyond human limits." He gestures towards the hooded figure. "A perfect example of what we can create."

Red Hat chuckles, adjusting his cuffs. "And I assume he's fully house-trained? No nasty surprises?"

The sharp-eyed man in the dark suit answers this time, his tone flat. "He's a controlled specimen. He responds to orders."

"Controlled?" Red Hat raises an eyebrow. "I like my investments to be predictable. Not sure what he is like though, he looks too small. I want someone big and strong, Intimidating but not too... obvious"

Dr. Heckingbottom's smirk widens. "You'll find he's

159

more than worth it. Enhanced strength, heightened senses, regenerative abilities. The perfect soldier, assassin, or enforcer. We have other subjects however, if he's not for you."

"That's the sort of thing I'm looking for." He replies. He gestures toward a metal case on the table.

"And you'll find the cost is fair for something so... rare." Heckingbottom runs his hands through his hair.

Red Hat steps forward, placing a gloved hand on the case. "I do love a good bargain." He flips the case open, revealing neatly stacked bundles of cash. "I don't want this one though. I want the Brute. You know, the one that's been making all the headlines lately."

Dr. Heckingbottom replies "Oh this one has made some headlines aswell. Did you not hear about the massacre at Black Water Farm? That was him."

The posh man interrupts, just as Red Hat was about to reply. "I received my own product a few months ago, at The Black Veils recommendation. He's incredibly strong."

Red Hat chuckles. "If this one is so good then why don't you buy it? I want the Brute. I've always had a fascination with Bears."

The sight makes my stomach twist. They are selling people. Experimenting on them. Turning them into weapons. And the bear is one of their experiments?

Joe shifts beside me, his foot scraping slightly against the wooden pallet. The sound is barely audible, but in the silence of the factory, it is enough. Every head turns. My heart stops.

Heckingbottom narrows his eyes, staring directly at me. He then turns to the hooded figure. "Find out what that was."

The figure lifts his head slightly. His face is still hidden, but something about the way he moves sends a chill through me. He hesitates for a moment, and I almost thought he'd seen us. Then his body tenses, muscles shifting.

His hood slips back, revealing a pale face. It's Kade. He looks different, almost… evil.

His bones crack and his limbs start elongating. His fingers curl into claws as dark fur erupts from his skin. His eyes burn bright red as his nose twitches, sniffing the air. He has turned into a werewolf. His gaze snaps towards our hiding spot. He starts moving toward us.

TWENTY-SEVEN
Duncan

While the prospect of blending human DNA with that of prehistoric creatures or modern animals stirs the imagination, it ventures into a realm where science dances with hubris. The ethical and biological complexities are staggering, yet, who is to say what future generations might achieve, or indeed, regret?"

- **Quote from Project Genesis by Professor Evelyn Harrington, Genetic Evolutionary Studies, 1997**

Kade's red eyes lock onto our hiding spot, his massive form shifting as he sniffs the air. My breath hitches. The low rumble in his throat scares me.

"Run," I whisper.

Joe and Aaron don't need to be told twice. We bolt from our cover, tearing across the factory floor to the door we came from. Behind us, Kade lets out a guttural snarl and launches forward, claws scraping against the concrete.

We sprint towards the door, shoving it open just as Kade's claws swipe through the air where we'd been moments before. Beyond the door is the kitchen. I don't have time to think. I dive towards the nearest hiding spot. It's the massive, dented rubbish dispenser. It reeks of spoiled food and discarded packaging. My stomach churns as I wriggle inside, forcing

162

myself down beneath the filth. The stench is unbearable, but it is my best chance. My only chance.

From a narrow crack between the bin's lid and the side, I can see the room, though barely. Joe scrambles towards a row of cabinets, yanking open the nearest one and squeezing himself inside. Aaron hesitates for just a second too long. I see his eyes flick to the window we climbed through, the only real way out.

He makes a break for it but Kade is faster. The werewolf lunges, slamming Aaron against the wall before he can reach the window. Aaron gasps for air, struggling, but Kade only tightens his grip. He leans in, sniffing deeply, before letting out a growl. He can't speak like this, his throat only capable of these deep, primal snarls, but his intent is clear. Aaron is trapped.

Kade's grip is getting tighter and tighter making Aaron's face go pale, his arms falling to his side, motionless.

Joe holds his breath in the cabinet, his body is pressed against the metal panels. I can't see him fully, but through the small opening in my hiding place, I see the faint creak as he shifts ever so slightly. Too slightly.

Kade's ears twitch. His head snaps toward the cabinet. He stalks forward, each step slow and deliberate. My pulse pounds as I watch his claws reach out.

Joe barely has time to react before the door is ripped off its hinges. He yelps as Kade drags him out, lifting him effortlessly.

The door we came through bangs open again. Heckingbottom and a few others from the meeting step inside.

"What's going on?" one of them demands.

Kade doesn't respond. He simply turns and shoves Joe forward. Joe lands hard, coughing as he scrambles back against the floor.

Dr. Heckingbottom takes a step forward, frowning as he studies Joe. "They were spying." His voice is calm, but there is something dangerous underneath it.

"Where's the other one? There were three of them that bolted for the door," says Langford.

"I saw him, that was the boy who came into my building the other week. His name is Duncan. If he ran, he couldn't have gone far." says Heckingbottom. "Go. Find where he lives, he's bound to scurry home at some point." He adds, staring at one of the men.

"What do we do with him?" asks the man in the suit jacket, pointing at Joe.

"This" Red Hat replies, pulling out a pistol and aiming it at Joe.

I can't watch. I bow my head down and close my eyes. The sound of a gunshot echoes through the room. I can feel tears forcing through my closed eyes. How could I let this happen, why did I get them involved.

The man in the red top hat chuckles. "Dispose of them, obviously."

I press myself slightly deeper into the bin, rotting food squishing beneath me. The stench is unbearable, thick and cloying, burning my throat. But I welcome it. It's the only thing keeping me hidden. My chest is tight, every breath shallow. If I breathe too hard, if I even shift slightly, he'll hear me.

Did they hear that? Kade, if I can still call him that, turns his head slightly, nostrils flaring. He sniffs the air again, his ears twitching. My body goes rigid. He is close. So close. I swear I can feel the heat radiating from him, the weight of his presence pressing down on me like a vice. Then, he hesitates. His nose wrinkles, his ears flatten just slightly. The putrid smell, God, it's unbearable, seems to bother him. And then, just like that, he steps back. He doesn't look my way again.

164

I don't let myself relax. I can't. Heckingbottom gives a nod. Two men grab Joe and Aaron. Dragging them like they're nothing more than sacks of meat.

I bite down hard on my lip, but it doesn't stop the sob from rising in my throat. My vision blurs. I squeeze my eyes shut, but the tears come anyway, hot and relentless, streaking my filthy face. My friends. They're gone. I want to scream. I want to run at them, to do something, anything—But I don't move. I don't breathe. The door swings shut behind them. And still, I wait.

Seconds stretch into minutes. My pulse hammers so hard I think it might give me away. My whole body trembles, my fingers digging into my arms so tightly that my nails cut into my skin. The kitchen is silent now, except for the faint dripping of a broken pipe somewhere in the room.

A choked sob escapes me before I can stop it. I press a filthy hand against my mouth, my shoulders shaking. Joe. Aaron. Their faces flash in my mind. Aaron's nervous laugh, Joe's stupid jokes. The way they made all of this feel less terrifying. They're gone. And I did nothing. I should've done something.

I squeeze my eyes shut again, swallowing back the bile rising in my throat. My fingers find the rim of the bin as I push myself up through the filth, shaking so hard I can barely keep myself steady. My limbs feel weak, like they might give out at any second.

My only way out is the window. I don't think. I just act. One last glance at the door, then I haul myself up and slip through, disappearing into the courtyard, alone.

TWENTY-EIGHT
Marlon

I wake with a sharp intake of breath, my body jerking upright as if I've been drowning in a nightmare. For a moment, I don't know where I am. The scent of stale coffee and faint cigarette smoke clings to the air. The battered leather sofa beneath me creaks as I shift. It clicks, I am in Dante's flat.

My brother is already up, standing near the window with his phone in hand. Dressed in his usual dark jeans and a plain black T-shirt, looking just like the undercover cop that he is. He turns when he hears me move.

"You're up," he says, slipping his phone into his pocket. "Good. You gonna tell me why you showed up at my door last night looking like hell?"

I frown, my memory is a bit foggy. "I... I was at Lanesworth's manor," I say hesitantly. "Something happened, Dante. You have to listen to me—"

"No," he cuts in sharply, shaking his head. "You were attacked by a bear not even a week ago, Marlon. You still haven't gotten over it. You turn up here, barely conscious, and passed out at my door. I don't know what you think happened last night, but I'm telling you, it's not real."

"It is! Why can't you help me, you're a cop. Can you not start digging into this shit aswell?" Dante works in the police station in a neighboring city. It is under a different

166

county so we rarely interact with each other at work.

He looks at me with a blank expression, he's definitely not going to help me. "It was real," I insist, gasping as I sit up. "I saw things. There was a man—"

Dante sighs, rubbing a hand down his tied back cornrows. "Enough. You need to get your head straight. Come on. I'm grabbing us some lunch, and you're coming with me. You need to clear your head and to stop pretending like it's you against the world."

I clench my jaw and hold my tongue. There is no point arguing, not yet. Maybe I can get him to go to Tony's Pizza. Duncan said he'd been speaking to him about the disappearances. Maybe if we go there, he'll let me talk to him about it.

"You've got a deal... on one condition." I say, forcing a smirk.

"Oh yeah, what's that?"

"I fancy pizza, haven't had one in a while."

"You're lucky I don't celebrate Easter. What about Tony's?" He asks, almost reading my mind.

"You got it." I chuckle.

The drive to Tony's Pizzas is quiet at first. I watch the city roll past the window, the early afternoon sun casts long shadows over the streets. The sounds of traffic and pedestrians fade into the background, my thoughts tangle with last night's events. I have barely processed everything, and now Dante is acting like none of it has even happened.

He turns on the radio, a low hum of classic rock fills the car. After a few moments, he sighs. "You're not saying anything. That's a bad sign."

"I'm thinking."

"About what?"

"What if I'm not crazy?" I mutter. "What if something

really happened to me?"

Dante taps his fingers against the steering wheel. "You're not crazy, Marlon. You just haven't dealt with what happened to you with the bear. And until you do, you're gonna keep seeing things that aren't there. It's gotta be some sort of paranoia, PTSD or schizophrenia."

I turn to stare out the window, my gut telling me he's wrong.

When we arrive at Tony's, my stomach drops. The entire front of the restaurant is sectioned off with police tape. A couple of officers stand near the entrance, talking to each other while the usual lunch crowd gathers at a distance, murmuring among themselves.

Dante mutters a curse under his breath. "What the hell happened here?"

We park in the car park across the street, and I step out first, approaching a woman who's standing near the edge of the gathered crowd. She looks familiar, probably a regular at Tony's.

"Hey," I say, trying to keep my voice calm. "What happened?"

She turns to me, her expression grim. "Antonio," she says quietly. "They say he had a heart attack last night. Didn't make it."

"A heart attack?"

"That's what they're saying," she murmurs. "But Antonio was fine yesterday. You know how strong he is."

I glance at the restaurant again. Something isn't right. He was digging into this mess just like I've been.

Dante puts a hand on my shoulder. "Come on, let's go. We'll try somewhere else"

I hesitated. I need to check on Duncan. I need to make sure he's okay. God knows what we've gotten ourselves into. I pull out my phone and dial his number, but no answer.

"We need to pop somewhere first. Duncan, he was looking into this just like Antonio. I don't buy that whole heart-attack story."

"So that's why you wanted to come here then? Because he was gonna convince me... Marlon, I told you, you have to let go." Dante's eyes look agitated and annoyed.

"He's just a boy Dante." I look into his eyes, pleading.

"Fine, but then we're grabbing lunch," he replies.

The drive to Duncan's house feels slower, like the air has thickened with tension. I stare out the window, my mind racing. Antonio's death doesn't sit right with me. The timing, the circumstances, it's too much of a coincidence.

Dante sighs beside me. "You're doing that thing again."

"What thing?"

"Getting all quiet, like you're trying to solve the world's biggest mystery."

"Maybe I am."

Dante shakes his head but doesn't push further. The tires hum against the road, the soft rhythm of the drive doing nothing to calm my nerves. Every street we pass feels like it is leading us deeper into something I'm not prepared for.

When we finally pull up near Duncan's house there isn't much room to park so we settle for somewhere about twenty meters down the street. I feel a strange weight settle in my chest. The street is quiet from traffic. For a moment, it seems normal.

Then, as I scan the area, I spot him. The man from Lanesworth's manor. Tall, broad-shouldered, built like a tank. He sits on Duncan's front door step, scanning the street as if waiting for someone.

A slow wave of unease creeps over me. I duck lower in

169

my seat, my pulse quickening. "Dante," I whisper. "Do you see him?"

Dante exhales sharply. "Yeah... I see him. Who the hell is that?"

Before either of us can decide on our next move, my phone rings. The sudden noise makes us both jump. I glance at the screen. It's Duncan.

I answered immediately. "Duncan?"

There is silence for a beat, then a whisper: "Marlon, I think someone's coming for me. Joe and Aaron are dead. I don't know what to do."

TWENTY-NINE
Duncan

I run through the thick vegetation, nettles and overgrown bushes slapping against my legs. "Marlon, they're coming for us. It's all linked, the attacks, that company, the disappearances."

Marlon's voice crackles through my phone "Duncan, you need to listen to me, don't go home." He sounds panicked and nervous, a side of him that I've never seen before. "There's a guy at your house, I've seen him before."

"He's with the group Marlon. I'm telling you, it's all connected. One of them was that Blackthorne guy. Heckingbottom was also there."

"How do you know?"

I nearly trip on a stray branch, hidden under some leaves. Steadying myself I say "I was at this warehouse, Kade was there, but he wasn't Kade. They're experimenting on people, Marlon."

"Jesus, those sick fucks. Alright where are you? We're coming to get you."

"Some old warehouse, up towards Eldemere." I struggle to catch my breath, I don't know if anyone saw me escaping the factory and I don't want to wait to find out. "I can meet you on Rustwood Road."

"Yeah, that works, we'll get there as fast as we can."

171

The wait on the side of the road feels like forever. I'm hiding behind a fallen long. I don't know who will be using this road, so I don't want to stand out. The smell of rotting wood and pine fills my nostrils. My already stinking clothes have gotten even more dirty as I lay down. I can't afford to be seen.

I can see the body of a car coming over the hill. The low hum of the engine makes my chest tighten. I get up and step closer to the road as a black car slows down.

The window rolls down, and Marlon's face appears, his sharp eyes scanning me. "Jesus Christ, Duncan. What the hell happened to you?" He wrinkles his nose. "You stink."

Dante, sitting in the driver's seat, leans out the window, squinting. "Did you roll in a dead animal or something?"

I don't have the energy to be embarrassed. I yank the door open and climb in, slumping against the seat. "I hid in a bin."

"What?" Marlon asks, the car pulls back onto the road.

"To get out. To escape." I swallow, the taste of bile still fresh in my throat. "It was that or die. Joe and Aaron couldn't hide quick enough." I start to break down again.

The car goes quiet except for the low hum of the engine. I try to compose myself and let out a shaky breath while pushing my damp hair back. "Kade was there. In the factory. But he wasn't... he wasn't human. He turned into some sort of werewolf. Like the things of legends. He killed Aaron. Tore him apart right in front of me."

Marlon curses under his breath, while Dante tightens his grip on the wheel, his jaw clenching.

"And that's not even the worst of it," I continue, forcing the words out. "There was a whole group of them, experimenting on people. They have prisoners. Lab rats. I don't know how many. I saw Heckingbottom, Blackthorne there. And this guy in a red hat, he shot Joe."

Marlon's expression darkens, but he doesn't interrupt, so I keep going. "Heckingbottom said that it's not Chimera that is involved with the disappearances. It sounded like that place was more of a front. Like he's using it. They mentioned the name The Black Veil. Sounded like that was the group's name. There was another name aswell. Langford. I've seen her before."

Marlon inhales sharply. He scratches his head. "Langford?"

"Yeah. You know her? Bossy looking, blonde hair."

Marlon exhales through his nose. "Jesus. Yeah, she's police. I don't know how deep this goes, but if she's involved in this..." He shakes his head. "We can't tell anyone. Not yet. We don't know how high up this goes. If Langford's in on it, others might be too. We can't trust anyone."

A lump forms again in my throat. I already know we are in trouble, but hearing Marlon say it makes it real. "They know about us," I admit. "They know we've both been looking into things. You, me, they're coming for us. We're not safe."

Marlon doesn't say anything right away. He keeps his eyes on the road as Dante drives, his jaw working like he is chewing over what to do next. Finally, he speaks. "We're picking up Latisha. Then we'll find somewhere to lay low. Give your Mum a call, make sure she's safe."

I nod, rubbing my arms as a shiver runs through me, despite the heat outside. I pull my phone out and stare at the screen for a second before calling my Mum. She picks up on the third ring.

"Duncan? You okay?" Her voice is filled with concern.

"I'm fine," I lie. "I just... I need to see you. Can you meet me after work? I'll tell you where later."

There is a pause, then, "Duncan, what's going on? You sound—"

"Please, Mum. Just meet me. I'll explain everything then."

Another pause. Then a sigh. "Okay. After work. I've still got a bit of work to do so I'm not sure when I'll finish. I knew I shouldn't have gone in today, it was double pay, I'm sorry."

"Mum it's fine, I'll see you in a bit."

I hang up, resting my head against the seat. My whole body aches, my clothes reek, and my mind is spinning, but I am alive. For now. We have to figure out what the hell to do next.

THIRTY
Marlon

They followed me to Hearthwick. I tried to warn this Italian guy about the bad group. I found they used a company called Chimera Solutions as a cover aswell as other things. They found out I was digging so I had to leave. I hope they don't go after him.

- ***Unknown Journal entry — Sunday, 20th April 2025***

I lead the group into my friend's house, the warm glow of the living room lamps makes it feel like a safe haven from everything happening outside. My friend, Kyle, stands in the doorway, arms crossed, a skeptical expression on his face. This isn't the most ideal option for a safe house but it's one of my only ones.

"So, let me get this straight," Kyle says, his eyes narrowing. "You're telling me that werewolves are real, and one of you is actually dealing with this… situation?"

I sigh, rubbing the back of my neck. "Look, I know it sounds insane, but we don't have time to argue about what's real and what's not. We need your help."

Kyle exhales sharply, shaking his head. "Man, I don't know… This sounds like something out of a bad movie."

Latisha steps forward. "Look, we wouldn't be here if it wasn't serious."

Kyle studies us for a moment before finally sighing. "Fine. I'll help. But don't expect me to start believing in monsters just yet."

I sit hunched over his desktop computer, my eyes scanning the screen while my fingers fly over the keyboard. Dante stands behind me, arms crossed, his presence a steady weight at my back. Latisha is on the sofa, phone in hand, but I can tell she is listening.

I type *'The Black Veil'* into the search bar. The screen lights up with vague nonsense. Some gothic poetry, a theatre production, and a bunch of conspiracy blogs linking the name to everything from cults to alien abductions. Typical internet rabbit hole stuff.

One link catches my eye. An old newspaper scan, dated 1897: *'The Black Veil: Secret Society or Folklore?'*

I click on it. It talks about a group supposedly active in Victorian-era London. Whispers of missing people, strange figures in long coats seen dragging bodies into carriages, and bizarre science experiments hidden beneath abandoned buildings. But it reads more like urban legend than evidence. No names, no locations, nothing I can actually use.

"Nothing concrete, just stories from Victorian times. Not sure if it's the same group but if it is then they go back centuries." I mutter, running a hand through my hair.

Dante stands behind me, arms folded, looking over my shoulder. "You thought they'd have a homepage or something?" he says, smirking. "Apply now to join your local secret society?"

I give him a side glance. "I was hoping someone online might've dug something up. I mean, if they've been doing this for over a hundred years, someone else must've noticed something."

Latisha looks up from her phone. "So what do we

actually know?"

I reply, "So we think they're called The Black Veil, and from what Duncan told me in the car they're experimenting on people. Who knows how many."

Dante butts in, "So we already know about three."

"Three?" Latisha asks. "So they've got Kade who's some sort of werewolf and some massive prehistoric looking bear, who else?"

"That Sophia chick. It was Antonio's wife." Dante replies.

I scratch my head. "We don't even know what's happened to her, only that she went missing."

"C'mon man. You really think she's not been tested on?" Dante asks, shaking his head.

"You can't think like that, we have to hope she's not."

I take a breath, trying to pull all the pieces together. "Duncan mentioned someone came to Tony's Pizza a while ago and warned him. No idea if she was connected to all this, but it's something. And we know this group's got money behind it. Buyers, investors, or whatever you wanna call them. Like the guy in the red top hat or possibly Lanesworth. He was at the auction, and he's loaded. They've got their hands in all sorts of places; Chimera Solutions, the police, who knows where else."

On the sofa, Latisha glances up from her phone. "Didn't you already look into Chimera Solutions? Was there anything else on there that might give us a clue?"

"Yeah," I say, turning back to the screen. "I went as deep as I could. Their public face is clean. Labs, research grants, community projects. Nothing that screams 'evil experiments.' But we know what they're really doing. Or at least, part of it. Duncan also told me that when he showed up there, they said there was some sort of hack going on. I bet that was some sort of cover-up to hide it from the rest of the staff

177

and the media."

Dante steps closer, eyeing the article. "If this Black Veil's been around that long, they're probably the kind of people who don't leave digital footprints. Old money. Real secretive. Probably got half the internet scrubbed."

Latisha tilts her head. "What about searching for werewolves? If that's what Kade has turned into then it might be good to know what we're dealing with?"

I start typing. I barely glance up when I hear Duncan's footsteps behind me. "Duncan, we're looking up everything we can on werewolves," I mutter.

Duncan, fresh out of the shower and still dripping, peers over my shoulder. The webpage displays an old, yellowed manuscript with a faded sketch of a half-transformed man; clawed hands, elongated fangs, and wild, inhuman eyes. The text beneath the image read:

'The curse of the lycanthrope is one that has plagued mankind for centuries. Those afflicted by the bite of a werewolf are doomed to transform fully under the full moon, their bodies twisted into creatures of the night, their minds overtaken by animalistic rage. There is no known cure... save for one.'

I scroll down, revealing a medieval woodcut of a village under attack by a massive wolf-like creature. My gut clenches. This is real. Too real.

"This site's got a ton of old records," I mutter, mostly to myself. "Books, myths, even some first-hand accounts."

Dante shifts beside me as I click another link, bringing up an aged document written in Old English. The translation beside it reads:

'A man, once infected, is doomed to bear the mark of the beast. Silver, the bane of such creatures, mayst bring them low, but a cure is rare and difficult. Legends speak of the Lycantheum Elixir, a concoction crafted from nature's own

deadly remedies. Should the beast be subdued, the potion might strip the curse from its veins.'

My jaw tightens. A cure. Kyle, standing behind us now, scoffs. "You're seriously buying into this? You think some medieval potion is gonna fix your werewolf problem?"

Dante leans in. "Lycantheum Elixir? What the hell is that?"

I click on another link, and this time, the page looks far more modern and official.

'The only known cure for lycanthropy is the Lycantheum Elixir. The afflicted must be incapacitated first—silver being the only proven means of neutralizing a werewolf. Once unconscious, the potion must be administered immediately.

The ingredients listed are:

Aconitum (Wolfsbane) *– Known for its poisonous properties, it is deadly in large doses but has been linked to folklore remedies.*

Garlic *– Traditionally used against supernatural creatures, it is believed to weaken a werewolf's strength.*

Bloodroot *– A plant used in ancient medicine, known for purging impurities from the blood.*

Mandrake Root *– A powerful herb often used in mythical transformations and counter-curses.'*

"For something so make-believe, this actually seems legit," Latisha mutters, peering over from the sofa. "And it's the only thing we've found that even mentions a cure."

Kyle huffs. "Yeah, legit like those websites that tell you vampires run the government."

I lean back, rubbing my chin. "So, silver bullet to take him down, then this potion."

Dante cracks his knuckles. "I can get a gun, I know a guy who sells them, blackmarket. He might have silver bullets also. This shouldn't be too hard."

I nod. "Do it. We need to be ready as soon as possible." I turn to Duncan. "You're in charge of getting the ingredients for the potion. I assume we already have garlic, probably laying in one of the kitchen cupboards, but we need Bloodroot, Mandrake root, and Aconitum."

Duncan blinks. "You want me to just... find those? Where am I even supposed to look? It's Easter Sunday for crying out loud!"

Latisha taps on her phone, already searching. "There's an old herbalist shop not far from here. They sell rare plants, including Aconitum and Mandrake root. Bloodroot might be tougher, but some apothecaries stock it. Says here that they're still open."

Kyle sighs again, rubbing his forehead. "Guys this is too much. I just don't buy it. Werewolves, what next, Vampires? Aliens? I'm gonna call Hewitt from work, he'll love this."

"Kyle don't, we don't really know we can trust. Don't tell anyone from work." I say. I can't let the police know. Langford's already involved in this. Who else? Hewitt? Stephens? It could be anybody.

"Fine I won't" Kyle replies with a small grin. I don't really trust him to keep this but I don't have much choice. Hopefully we can be gone and out of his hair before he tells anyone.

"You need to speak to your Mum later" I say, nodding at Duncan. "We don't know if they're aware of where she works, we can't take chances."

"Thanks" he replies.

I exhale, running a hand over my face. "Alright. We don't have much time. Let's get moving."

THIRTY-ONE
Duncan

The small bell above the door of the herbalist shop rings as my trainers meet the tattered old doormat. The wooden door closes behind me, making a small shud sound. The air smells fresh, a mix of citrus, spice and a tang of orange.

"You're lucky, ten more minutes and we'd be closing. Can I help you?" The innocent voice of an elderly asian lady passes through the shop from the counter as she chuckles to herself. Her frame looks small and fragile.

"I'm just looking for a few bits, I've got a list on some paper. Would you be able to help?"

I pass her the scrunched up note that I marked up while at Kyle's house. I'd never heard of the stuff they've asked me to get so I didn't want to run the risk of forgetting. Luckily there is no one else in the shop so I have the ladies' full attention.

She brushes back her long grey hair over her shoulder, it is put in a ponytail however it had drooped over her front.

Lowering her small rounded glasses from atop her head she squints as she looks at the note. "Ah, Aconitum... also called wolfsbane. It's very toxic, so be careful. We only sell it diluted, but even then, gloves are best. My father used it for pain relief when I was a child."

"It's poisonous to touch?" I take half a step back.

181

"A little. Ah mandrake root... powerful stuff. Some fools try to use it recreationally, but I don't recommend it. It's also diluted down, but still, handle it carefully."

Rubbing my hand over the back of my neck I reply "I wasn't planning on it."

"Legends say that because the root looks human-like, it lets out a scream when pulled from the ground."

The shopkeeper reaches down to pick up a key to unlock the locked cabinet behind the counter. "And Bloodoot?" she questions, glancing at the paper in her other hand as she is unlocking the cabinet. "What are you making?" Her now-cautious eyes give me a look of distrust, as she questions my morals.

"Oh, it's for a school project on historical herbal medicine. We're supposed to research old remedies and superstitions, and I thought I'd get real samples." I can't believe that I thought of that on the spot and said it so confidently.

"Oh... I see. Historical herbal medicine? They're letting students handle aconitum now?"

"Well..." I pause for a moment, gathering my train of thought. "I just want to get a better feeling of its benefits, I'm a very visual learner."

"Okay..." She seems hesitant but gives in to my lie. "Are there any other herbs that you are looking for?"

"That should be it, thank you. How much is that?" I say, scratching my head.

"£25 for the Aconitum, £15 for the Mandrake, and £8 for the Bloodroot. So in total that's £48." Her eyes glance up at me, probably not expecting me to be able to pay for it.

Luckily Latisha and Dante both gave me some cash beforehand so I hand over fifty pounds.

Carrying a small brown paper bag I exit the shop, the

182

small bell chimes out again as I pass through the door. My phone starts to buzz, my Mum's name flashing on the screen.

"Hey, Mum," I say, trying to sound casual even though I can feel the weight of everything pressing down on me.

"Duncan," she replies, her voice is tired but concerned. "I just finished work. So, where am I supposed to meet you? You didn't exactly tell me much earlier."

I rub the back of my neck, already knowing this is going to be tough. "Yeah, I know. I'm sorry. Listen, I need you to meet me at Kyle's place. It's important."

There is a pause on the other end. "Kyle? Who's Kyle? You never mentioned him before."

I sigh. "I know, I know. I met him today. He's someone I'm working with... Look, I can't explain everything right now. But just trust me on this. I need you to meet me at 22 Harrow Way."

"22 Harrow Way?" she repeats, clearly confused. "You want me to go to some random address? And I don't even know who Kyle is, Duncan."

"I know it sounds crazy, but please, Mum, just do this. It's important," I say, the urgency in my voice growing.

"Duncan, you sound paranoid. Are you in trouble? Who is this Kyle?"

"He's a friend, Mum. But... there's one more thing. You have to make sure you're not being followed. Don't take any chances, alright? Don't let anyone tail you."

She goes silent for a second. I can hear her breathing, processing what I am saying. "This sounds insane, Duncan," she mutters. "But fine. I'll go. But you better explain what's going on when I get there. 22 Harrow Way. But if I'm being followed, I swear..."

"I promise, I'll explain everything soon. Just be careful, okay? If anything feels off, don't go there."

"I will, but you're not making this easy, you know that?" she says, her voice softening a little.

"I know. I'm sorry. I'll see you soon."

"Alright, Duncan. Be safe. I'll be there."

THIRTY-TWO
Marlon

"A silver bullet will kill a werewolf, sure. But if you think that's all it takes, you've already lost. A wounded wolf is still a wolf, and a desperate one is twice as deadly."
- **Elias Blackthorne, Veteran Monster Hunter, 1459 AD**

The quiet alley off Craydon Street is the perfect meeting spot, tucked away from prying eyes, shielded by tall brick buildings that loom over. The air smells of damp stone and old rubbish, the kind of place where people do business they didn't want others to know about. A battered metal door stands ajar at the far end alley, an open invitation to those who know where to look.

Dante and I approach cautiously, checking over our shoulders before stepping inside. The room is dimly lit, a single flickering bulb swaying slightly from the ceiling. Stacks of wooden crates line the walls, some marked with strange symbols, others left blank. The faint scent of grease and tobacco clings to the air, mixing with the sharp tang of gunpowder.

Obsidian is already waiting, perched on a wooden crate like he had all the time in the world. He is a wiry man, all sharp edges and restless energy, his dark leather trench coat hangs off his frame like a second skin. His slicked-back hair glistens under the weak light, and fancy silver rings adorn nearly every one of his fingers, catching the dim glow as he taps them idly against the crate. He has a face that could be charming or menacing, depending on the angle of the light. Right now, it is a bit of both.

"Didn't expect two cops today," Obsidian says, his voice rough like gravel. "Business or pleasure?"

I step forward, keeping my hands where he can see them. "Like Dante said on the phone, we need a pistol with a loaded full magazine and a few silver bullets."

Obsidian raises an eyebrow, a slow smirk tugging at his lips. "Silver, huh? Now that's interesting. You expecting trouble from something... unnatural?"

"Just a precaution," Dante says, his tone even. He told me on the way here that he never liked dealing with Obsidian, but we both knew this guy has what we need. "Do you have it or not?"

Obsidian chuckles, shaking his head. "Always so serious. Lighten up boys, you make it sound like I'm about to sell you something... illegal." He lets out another laugh, then reaches into a crate behind him. With a theatrical flourish, he pulls out a sleek black pistol. It is well-maintained, the grip slightly worn but sturdy. He places it on the table between us, then reaches into his coat and withdraws a small velvet pouch, pinching it between two fingers.

He holds it up, letting the weak light reflect off the polished silver bullet inside. "Handcrafted. Pure silver. Not exactly standard issue, but it'll get the job done, if you hit your mark."

"Only one?" I reply.

Obsidian schoffs. "Silver bullets aren't all that common funnily enough. Count yourself lucky that I managed to get one."

I exchange a glance with Dante, who gives me a slight nod. He doesn't like doing business with Obsidian, but sometimes the devil you know is better than the one you don't. I reach into my coat, pulling out a bundle of cash that I withdrew on the journey here. Obsidian snatches it from my hand, flipping through the notes with quick, practiced movements before stuffing them into his pocket.

"Pleasure doing business," he says smoothly. "Try not to make a mess."

Dante pockets the pistol, and I take the bullet carefully, tucking it into my coat. With one last glance at the dealer, we turn and walk out the door, the transaction completed.

Once we are back in the car, Dante's work phone buzzes. He frowns, glancing at the screen. It is a number from the station.

"Yeah?" he answers, already knowing he won't like what is coming next.

"Dante, we need you to check out a situation," a tired voice on the other end says. "There's been a disturbance on the outskirts of the next town over, it's Brackstead. You know, the run-down industrial place on the outskirts of the city. It used to be the indoor skatepark, it's just opposite there. Apparently there's busted doors, shorted-out streetlights... witnesses are saying it's like a walking power surge."

I glance at my brother as he processes the information. "This late on a Friday? I wasn't even supposed to be working today."

"Yeah, well, we're short on staff. Can you handle it?"

Dante lets out a long sigh, rubbing the bridge of his nose. "Fine. I'll check it out."

He hangs up and turns to me. "Sounds weird. Could be related to the experiments."

I nod, mulling it over. "Could be. Shall I head back to Kyle's while you check this out?"

Dante taps the steering wheel thoughtfully. "If it is related I might need you there. I know it's not protocol as you're a copper from a different county, but nothing about what we're doing is protocol. Also, we might want to keep this pistol to hand."

I exhale sharply, thinking about what we've just bought. "Good thing we got the silver bullet, then."

The car rumbles to life and we pull out of the alley.

THIRTY-THREE
Marlon

Brackstead is unusually quiet. The evening is starting to draw in as we roll down the road that the old skate park is located on. The streetlights bare only a flicker, unusual for this time. None of the houses nearby have lights on. With the exception of our car headlights, the only luminous thing is a few candles that we can see flickering through the window from the house to the left.

We pull over on the side of the road by the house, getting out cautiously. I can't help but feel something dangerous or paranormal is roaming these streets.

"Look at that!" Dante says, pointing over to the flickering streetlight. "If the power was totally out then it wouldn't even flicker. What the hell is going on?"

"Let's knock on some doors, see if anyone's seen anything." I suggest.

We walk up to one of the houses with the candles and Dante hits the doorbell. We can hear some movement inside but they don't open the door. Faint whispers seep through, too quiet to make out whatever the person on the other side is saying.

"It's the police, can you open up please?" Dante says with a raised authoritative voice.

The metallic sound of the key turning in the lock

chimes out and the door handle goes down, the door slowly opening. A head peeks through the gap.

"Sorry, We didn't want to open the door, we didn't know who you were." An old woman calls out in a worried tone, still hiding partly behind the door.

"Can you tell us what's happened?" Dante asks.

The woman looks a bit shocked when she first sees my face, battered and bruised. She keeps looking behind us, almost expecting something or someone to be out there. I can't help but keep glancing back myself, just to check.

I take a small step forward "Can you just tell us what you saw."

She shuffles back slightly as I approach. "I—I don't know what's happenin' out here," she starts, her voice a mix of fear and uncertainty. "Lights went out not long after sunset. Thought it was just another outage, it happens now and then, you know? But then... then I saw 'em. A group of them, men wearing masks, running down that road over there." She points a shaky finger toward the far side of the street.

Dante frowns. "What did they look like?"

"Dark clothes, moving fast, like they were after someone," The woman replies, her voice lowering. "And they were. There was a man. I couldn't see his face too well, but he wasn't dressed like them. They were chasing him, and I thought, 'Oh, Lord, he's in trouble,' but then..." She trails off, rubbing her hands together.

I lean in slightly. "Then what?"

She swallows hard. "Then there was this light. Bright and blue, like lightning, but it wasn't coming from the sky. It came from him" She nods in the direction the fight had happened, her eyes wide. "He turned, just for a second, and the air hummed. I felt it in my bones. Then, boom. A crack like a whip, and those masked men went flying back like they'd been kicked by a horse. Some of 'em got up, limping away, but they didn't try again. No sir, they ran."

Dante and I exchange a look. This isn't just some random guy in a fight, it has to be connected to the experiments. Some sort of power surge and brute force, this isn't normal.

"Where did the man go?" Dante asks.

She hesitates, glancing toward the abandoned industrial units. "I saw him after," she says, softer now. "He looked tired. Stumbled a little, but he kept moving. He went that way, toward the old auction house." She points past the flickering streetlights to a rundown building in the distance. "He might still be there. But you boys... be careful."

"Why?" I ask.

She shudders. "Because whatever he is, I don't think he's normal."

"Okay thank you ma'am. I suggest locking your doors for tonight. We're going to check this thing out and then try and get your power back on." Dante says, scratching his face.

As we walk back to the car I turn to Dante. "This has to be linked. It has to be."

He nods in approval. "Well let's go find out."

We hop back in Dante's car and start heading down the road towards the old building. It's not far, but having the car closer incase we need to bolt is a good idea.

The old auction house looms over us, a crumbling shell of its former self. The grand entrance is boarded up, and what little remains of the once-polished stone steps are now chipped and cracked, worn down by time and neglect. The windows are shattered in places, jagged glass catching the last remnants of daylight. No power. No movement. Just silence and the faint scent of damp wood and decay.

Dante and I approach cautiously, our footsteps

crunching against loose gravel and broken glass.

"Looks abandoned enough," I mutter.

Dante exhales sharply. "Yeah. Let's hope he's still here."

Finding a way in isn't hard. A side door, half off its hinges, gives way with a firm push. The interior is just as lifeless as the outside. The once-grand hall is now a graveyard of overturned chairs, rotting wooden podiums, and dust-covered drapery hanging limply from the ceiling. Shafts of dying moonlight barely piercing the gloom through cracks in the walls.

"Stay close," Dante murmurs as we move further in.

The silence is oppressive, thick like fog. Our footsteps echo against the high ceiling, making it feel like we aren't alone. The deeper we go, the darker it becomes. I pull out my phone, using its flashlight to cut through the shadows entering into one of the side rooms, I walk in alone. The beam sweeps across forgotten relics of past auctions; torn-up catalogues, old ledgers, broken furniture.

A noise slices through the still air, making me turn on the spot. It's a sharp, gut-wrenching scream. Dante's scream. My blood turns to ice.

"Dante!" I scramble towards the sound as quickly as my broken body lets me, shoving through a collapsed doorway.

In the next room, Dante is on his knees, frozen in place, a gun pressed to his temple. Holding the gun is a man who also looks like he's been through hell and barely crawled out. His clothes are torn, streaked with grime and dried blood. His dark hair is damp with sweat, his face gaunt and exhausted. But his eyes look wild and full of pain, they are locked onto me.

"You need to leave me the hell alone," the man growls. His hand is steady, but there is a tremor in his voice, a flicker of something deeper beneath the rage.

"Whoa, whoa!" I hold up my hands, taking a slow step forward. "We're not here to hurt you."

"Bullshit!" His grip tightens on the gun. "You think I don't know when I'm being hunted? Every damn time I try to stop running, more of you come after me!"

"We're not them!" I insist. "We're not—"

Before I can finish, he lunges at me.

I barely have time to react before he tackles me, knocking me straight into a pile of debris. The air rushes out of my lungs as we crash to the floor. The gun slips from his grip, skidding across the dusty floor. I struggle through the pain, trying to break free, but his grip is like steel.

Dante, scrambling to his feet, grabs the gun. "Back off!" he barks, aiming it at the man.

The man freezes, his breathing ragged. His hands are clenched into fists, but he doesn't make another move. His eyes flicker between me and the barrel of the gun, now pointed at him.

"We're not here to fight you," Dante says, his voice firm. "But we will defend ourselves."

The man's jaw tightens, but he doesn't advance. Slowly, he backs away, hands still clenched.

"Then what the hell do you want?" he asks, voice rough.

I hesitate. My mouth opens, then closes again. Should I say it? Saying the name feels like lighting a match in a room full of gasoline. I don't even know if this guy is linked to it, but if I want answers, I have to take the risk.

"We're looking for someone," I finally say. "A kid named Kade. And... we know about The Black Veil and Chimera Solutions."

His expression darkens instantly. "You know about

193

GONE BEFORE THE MOON

them?" His voice is almost a whisper, but there is nothing quiet about the rage simmering beneath it.

"Not everything," I admit. "But enough to know that they've hurt people. Experimented on them. And that Kade... he is one of them. isn't he?"

The man lets out a bitter laugh, shaking his head. "Yeah... yeah, he was. We all were." He runs a hand through his hair, exhaling sharply. "Some of us had volunteered for treatment at Chimera Solutions, some were just taken. I tried digging after I got out. It's all a cover up. There's a lab. Hidden. Deep in Blackwood Forest. That's where they kept us. Where they did things to us. Kade... he was there."

I feel my stomach drop. "Kept you? You mean—"

"Experiments," he interupts bitterly. "We weren't people to them. We were just projects. Test subjects."

I swallow hard. "And Kade? Where is he now?"

He shakes his head. "He helped me get out, but he didn't escape. I don't know where he is now, but if you're looking for him, that lab's your best bet."

Dante and I exchange a glance. This is bigger than we thought. We've been searching for Kade, but this? A whole lab of people like him?

I take a cautious step forward. "Come with us. Help us find him."

The man stiffens. "No."

"You know more than we do," Dante adds. "You could—"

"I said no!" His voice is sharp and final. "I'm done being part of this mess. I just want to be left alone."

There is no convincing him. He's already made up his mind. He looks between us once more, something unreadable in his eyes. Then, without another word, he turns and bolts for the nearest exit, disappearing into the growing night. I stand there, heart pounding, watching the last trace of him vanish into the darkness.

"Well," Dante mutters after a beat. "That went well."

I let out a slow breath, steadying myself. "At least we have a lead. The lab in Blackwood Forest."

Dante nods. "Yeah. But if his story is true… we're walking straight into a nightmare."

I glance at the empty doorway where he had just escaped, his words still ringing in my ears. "We weren't people to them. We were just projects."

I clench my fists. If that is true, then we have no choice. We have to find that lab. And we have to find Kade.

THIRTY-FOUR
Duncan

Tonight is the night we get Kade back. I don't want to just get him back, I want to make these people pay for what they've done. I don't know if I have the courage to do it though.
- ***Diary entry from Duncan Webb — Sunday, 20th April 2025***

A fog-like gas spews out of the saucepan, rising like a phantom before dispersing outwards. The recipe we're following online for Lycantheum Elixir doesn't mention using a saucepan in your mate's kitchen, but we're making do.

"This thing smells nasty," Latisha mutters, stirring the potion as she wafts away the mist curling around her. It's getting thicker, creeping along the ceiling like it's alive.

The heavy air clings to my throat, every breath a chore. I take that as my cue to step out of the room and get ready. We're heading to the cabin tonight, under cover of darkness. My Mum absolutely hates the idea, but there's no talking me out of it. Marlon and Dante are coming with me, and their police background is the only thing stopping her from locking the door.

As I walk out I cough once, then wave a hand in front of my face. "I'm gonna grab the rest of my stuff."

"Probably for the best," Kyle says, stepping in from the

hallway with a backpack slung over one shoulder. He hands it to me. "Here you go, kid. Not sure what you'll need, but take what you can find, Trust your gut."

"Thanks," I reply, my voice shaky with nerves.

I step further away from the kitchen, the fog clinging to my clothes as I pass through what's spewing out the room. I can hear Latisha behind me muttering something about needing better ventilation.

As I head down the hallway, the silence in the house feels heavier than before, like even the walls are holding their breath. My footsteps feel too loud on the floorboards as I open random drawers and cupboards. Cutlery. Cans. An unopened bottle of whiskey. Not exactly survival gear. I snag a few protein bars and shove them into the backpack.

Next stop, the hallway closet. A wave of dust greets me as I open the door. I dig through mismatched gloves, towels, and a heavy winter coat, finally finding a small flashlight tucked behind a stack of old books. I test it, and it still works. Batteries sit in a plastic tub nearby; I grab those too, along with a roll of duct tape. Might come in handy, even if I'm not sure how yet.

In Kyle's office, I find a pocket knife buried beneath a mess of paperclips and receipts. It feels cold and unfamiliar in my hand, but I slip it into my pocket anyway. My fingers shake a little.

As I step back into the hallway, I almost bump into Marlon. He still looks like hell, even after he's tried to clean himself up. He raises an eyebrow.

"Find anything good?"

"Some food, flashlight, batteries... and duct tape."

Marlon smirks. "Duct tape, huh? You planning on fixing a leaky pipe out there?"

I shrug. "They say it solves most problems."

He chuckles, then nods toward my pocket. "Keep that knife close. Just in case."

I give him a small nod. The weight of everything we're doing settles deeper into my chest.

I nod, and we head downstairs together. The living room is lit with a soft amber glow. Everyone's huddled around the coffee table. Latisha hands Marlon a small vial of shimmering dark blue liquid. Kyle is hunched over a freshly printed map of Blackwood Forest, marking search areas. Dante's loading gear. My Mum stands at the window, arms wrapped tightly around herself. Her eyes flick to me as I enter, and I can see the storm building inside her.

Kyle kneels over the map, smoothing it flat. "It's a full moon tonight. Might help visibility, but we need backup light just in case."

I step forward, setting down my small pile of supplies beside the map. "This is all I could find."

Before anyone can respond, my Mum speaks up.

"Really, Duncan?" Her voice is tight, barely holding together. "You've done enough. Just… let the adults go."

My eyes meet hers. "Mum, I know you're scared, but I need to do this."

She walks closer, not angry, just exhausted. "Do you hear yourself? You're sixteen. You shouldn't be packing bags like this. You should be at school. Or asleep in your bed. Not heading into the woods with—" her voice falters, "with God knows what out there."

I hesitate. The weight in my chest turns sharp.

"If it were me out there, Kade would go," I say quietly. "He wouldn't even hesitate."

She looks like I've slapped her. Her jaw trembles. "But it's not you out there. It's you here. With me. I'm your Mum, Duncan. It's my job to protect you."

198

"I know," I whisper. "But I'm not backing down."

She turns away, blinking fast. Her shoulders sag like she's deflating. "Then just... stay close to Marlon. Please. I love you."

"I will. I love you too."

Latisha stands up from the sofa, breaking the tension like cracking glass. "He's going to be okay. Just don't do anything reckless, alright?" She gives Marlon a sharp look. "And don't make me need to brew another one of these," she mutters, nodding to the shimmering vial.

Kyle moves toward me and holds out a black hoodie. "Here. Bit big on you, but it'll help you blend in better."

I slip it on. It's warm, heavier than expected. Safer, somehow.

Dante checks his pistol, fingers brushing over the silver bullet before tucking it into a coat pocket instead of the chamber. "We don't know what else is out there. We get close, use the potion, and bring Kade back. If we can."

Marlon adjusts his vest and pockets the vial. "We move out in five."

No more arguing. Just nods. Determination. The silence before a storm.

I glance once more at my Mum. Her hand rests on the windowsill, fingers pressed tight like she's holding herself back from grabbing me and locking the door.

I want to say something more. But I don't know what. So I say nothing. And we prepare to walk into the dark.

THIRTY-FIVE
Marlon

The trees press in around us, black silhouettes against a deep navy sky. The forest stretches out endlessly, a labyrinth of tangled branches and clawing undergrowth. Our headlights cut a narrow tunnel through the darkness, illuminating gnarled roots and the occasional flash of startled wildlife before vanishing into the void beyond.

The tires crunch over the dirt road, but the deeper we drive, the rougher the terrain becomes. The car jolts suddenly as we hit another pothole, and Dante grunts in frustration.

"This is as far as we go," he says, shifting the gear into neutral and pulling up the handbrake.

I exhale sharply, gripping the handle as I step out. The cold night air wraps around me, thick with the damp, earthy scent of decaying leaves. The forest is alive with distant noises; rustling foliage, the high-pitched cry of an owl and the whisper of the wind threading through the branches.

Dante pulls out a cigarette and lights it, taking a long drag before tossing his lighter towards me. "Sort yourself out."

I catch it against my chest and stuff it into my pocket, adjusting the straps of my bag. My hands are now full, one gripping my flashlight, the other resting near the knife on my belt. I turn to Duncan, who stands stiffly beside me. Even in the dim light, I can see the tension in his shoulders, the way his fingers twitch at his sides.

"You alright?" I ask.

Duncan nods quickly. "Yeah."

I'm not convinced. The kid is putting on a brave face, but his eyes dart toward the trees too often, scanning the shifting darkness like he's expecting something to leap out at any moment.

Dante motions ahead. "Let's move."

We step off the path, boots sinking into the damp earth. The deeper we venture, the heavier the darkness becomes. Towering pines and ancient oaks loom overhead, their skeletal branches twisting together like grasping fingers, hiding the slight light coming from the full moon. The air is thick with the scent of moss.

Duncan breaks the silence. "How much further?"

"Couple miles," Dante replies. "We'll make it in no time."

"If nothing finds us first," I mutter.

Duncan forces a chuckle, but I can hear the strain behind it. "Right. No big deal. Just a casual midnight hike through a haunted forest."

Dante smirks, adjusting the gun holster under his jacket. "You're getting it."

The conversation lulls, leaving only the sound of our footsteps and the occasional rustle of unseen creatures in the undergrowth. A sharp snap echoes from ahead. I freeze. Then another, closer this time.

I exchange a look with Dante, whose hand immediately goes to his gun. Duncan takes a step back, his breath hitching as he peers into the blackness between the trees.

The forest erupts. Something moves, fast. A blur of motion, a rush of heavy footfalls pounding against the earth. The undergrowth explodes as Duncan bolts, his panicked breath is loud in the stillness.

"Duncan!" I shout, but the kid is already gone, swallowed by the shadows.

Another snap echoes out, this time closer. Then the sound of a growl. Low, deep, a guttural rumble that sends a primal shiver down my spine. Something is hunting us.

"Move!" Dante barks.

Dante leads the charge as I hobble behind as quickly as my body lets me. We go to the right, in the direction that Duncan ran. We dodge low branches, our boots skidding over damp leaves and slick roots. The sound of pursuit crashes through the trees behind us. Heavy paws slam against the ground. A snarl that vibrates in my chest.

Dante grunts suddenly and falls forward. I turn just in time to see the shape. A huge, hulking mass of fur and muscle, it lunges out of the darkness.

It is massive, at least eight feet tall, covered in thick, matted fur. Its eyes burn bright red, glowing like embers in the night. A muzzle lined with jagged teeth twists into a snarl, saliva glistening as it bares its fangs. Claws, long and curved, gleaming in the dim light.

Dante barely has time to raise his arm before the werewolf strikes, its claws raking across his shoulder. He cries out, stumbling back as blood splatters across the leaves.

I don't hesitate. I step in quickly, slashing my knife across the creature's side. It barely flinches. The werewolf's head snaps toward me, lips peeling back in a vicious snarl. Before it can lunge, Dante fires a few shots with his ordinary bullets loaded. The gun kicks in his hands, the muzzle flash momentarily lighting up the beast's monstrous face. The werewolf recoils, not from pain but from surprise. It hadn't expected resistance.

"Run!" I grab Dante, shoving him forward as we

202

charge towards an opening.

My body feels on fire as we crash into a clearing. The remains of old stone walls offer some semblance of cover. I dig deep and haul Dante behind one, pressing him against the crumbling stone. Blood seeps from the deep gashes across his shoulder, but he is still conscious, still gripping his gun tightly. Branches snap in the distance. The werewolf starts circling us.

My breath comes fast and shallow as I peek over the ruins. The darkness beyond is shifting, moving. A low, guttural growl rumbles through the trees, a sound that speaks of hunger, of patience.

I take off my jacket, tying it around my brother's blood-covered shoulder to try and stop the bleeding. "You're gonna be alright kid, hold on." My hands start to shake. "Where's the silver bullet?"

Dante, struggling to get his words out says, "Pocket... It's in my trouser pocket."

My hands tremble as I reach in, searching for the bullet. I pull it out and grab the gun off him, loading the silver bullet in.

"We need to use these walls as cover. If this bastard wants to get us, he's going to need to come out of the cover of darkness. That's when I'm gonna shoot him."

THIRTY-SIX
Duncan

Beneath the silver hunter's eye,
Where shadows writhe and branches sigh,
The wolf's lament, a mournful cry,
Beware the beast that walks the night.
O children, heed your mother's plea,
Stay far from woods and ancient tree.
For where the forest whispers free,
The wolf's sharp teeth shall feast on thee.
- ***Poem From Noctis Umbra: Chronicles of the Darkened Moon by Father Gregor Petrov, 1483***

My breath is coming in frequent short actions, my heart working faster than it ever has before. I don't dare look back. Kade could be right on my tail. Vines are whipping my shins as I maneuver over fallen logs and nettles. The uneven ground is covered in leaves making it nearly impossible to safely traverse through. The little light given off by the full moon is being blocked by the tall oak trees, standing there like bodyguards.

I try to tell myself I'm not a coward, but maybe Mum was right. Maybe I should have just stayed at Kyle's house. I tell myself that I wasn't running away, I was running to find the cabin. The one with the lab hidden beneath it. That is what matters aswell. Marlon and Dante can hopefully give the potion to Kade and cure him. If I can find this lab , maybe I can stop these disappearances forever.

As I run I reach into my pocket, fumbling around for the pocket knife I found at Kyle's. I open it to reveal the small sharp blade, gripping it tightly in case something jumps out at me.

I slow my pace, squinting through the gloom. Just ahead is a break in the brush. As I approach I see flattened leaves, crushed twigs, and the faint imprint of tire tracks in the damp earth. I crouch down, running my fingers lightly over the ridges. They are fresh. Someone has driven this way recently. A van? An off-road vehicle? It doesn't matter. If there is a trail, I can follow it.

For a while, it's easy. The tracks weave between the trees, the ground still soft enough to hold their shape. But after a few minutes of following, they vanish. I freeze, scanning the forest floor. Have I taken a wrong turn? The mud thins here, giving way to roots and patches of wild grass. I turn in slow circles, my pulse rising. Has someone deliberately covered the tracks?

About ten meters ahead I spot a broken branch, just beyond a tangle of ferns. I push forward, finding the tracks again, though they are fainter now.

As I creep through the trees, the night presses in around me. The wind sighs through the branches, setting the leaves rustling. But then there is another sound. A snap, too sharp to be the wind. Is it the werewolf again? My fingers tighten around my pocket knife as I twist, scanning the darkness.

Nothing. Still, I move faster, my nerves on edge, until the trees thin again, and I see it. A cabin. It is smaller than I expected, hunched in the middle of a clearing like it has been dropped there and forgotten. The wooden walls are weathered and cracked, vines creeping up the sides. The windows are dark and lifeless, their glass smeared with dirt and grime. The roof sags slightly in places, barely holding itself together. To the left, a shed is slumped against the side of the cabin, its rusted corrugated metal roof barely clinging to the rotting wooden frame. I swallow hard. It looks abandoned. But that doesn't mean no one is here.

Moving carefully, I circle the cabin, searching for an easy way in. The doors are shut tight, the windows on the ground floor mostly boarded up or too grimy to see through. I glance up and see a window on the second floor, slightly ajar. If I can get up there, then that's my way in.

The shed is my best bet. I step onto the metal roof as lightly as I can, but the moment my weight shifts, the rusted sheets groan beneath me. I freeze. The sound echoes in the still night, making my breath hitch in my throat. I move slower, carefully crawling toward the cabin's side. Every shift of my weight makes the roof creak and bend, the metal brittle beneath me.

Finally, I reach the window. Praying it isn't locked, I push it open just enough to squeeze through and slip inside, landing softly on the wooden floor.

The air is stale, thick with dust and decay. Even in the darkness, I can see that the upstairs hallway is narrow and cramped, the walls lined with peeling wallpaper, its floral pattern barely visible beneath years of grime and mold. The wooden floor is warped, some planks slightly raised, others splintering at the edges. I grip my knife tighter.

Moving cautiously, I start checking the upstairs rooms. Most are empty, an old bed frame here, a tattered chair there. But there are signs of recent activity. A half-empty bottle of water on a nightstand. Faint boot prints in the dust near the doorway. Someone has been here. Maybe they still are.

Suddenly, the floorboards creak loudly beneath my feet. A loud, sharp sound in the silence. I barely have time to react before a door slams from downstairs.

I don't think, I just drop, rolling under the nearest bed, pressing myself into the shadows. The wooden slats above me are thick with cobwebs, the scent of old fabric and rotting wood fill my nose. I hold my breath, heart pounding as I listen.

THIRTY-SEVEN
Duncan

I press myself against the cold floor, my breath shallow as I try to quiet the hammering in my chest. The wooden boards beneath the bed feel unyielding, the air thick with dust and fear. My fingers tighten around the pocket knife that's now hidden behind my back, my last line of defense.

Footsteps, slow and deliberate. They reach the top of the stairs, pausing between each creak as if savoring the hunt. My pulse pounds in my ears as I hear doors opening, one after the other. Searching.

A door creaks open down the hall. Heavy boots step inside, a pause, then another door. My stomach tightens as whoever it is moves closer, checking each room with unhurried precision. They know someone is here.

Then, my door. The hinges groan as it swings open, and I see polished black boots step inside. A low, amused breath escapes the intruder.

"I know you're here," the voice says, smooth and dripping with menace. "Come out."

I squeeze my eyes shut. I know that voice. It's the same one from the factory. The same one who ordered Kade to be changed. The same one who stood there as Aaron and Joe were killed. Maybe the same one I'd been researching. Dr. Blackthorne.

A metallic click sounds from the man. My breath hitches as I spot the Glock in his hand, pointed at the floor but ready. "You shouldn't have been sniffing around, boy. You've seen too much. Your little crusade ends here."

I try to steady my breathing as I slowly slide out from under the bed, my hands trembling. My pocket knife presses into my palm, hidden behind my back. My voice wavers. "Please... you don't have to do this."

Blackthorne tilts his head, smiling like I amuse him. "Don't I? You and your little friends have been quite the nuisance. Do you know how many lives our work has changed, saved? And yet, you insist on getting in the way."

Tears burn at the edges of my eyes. "Kade isn't an experiment! He's my friend! You have to stop this. You have to give him back."

Blackthorne scoffs. "He's beyond saving."

"No! He's not!" My voice cracks. "You turned him into something he never wanted to be! And Aaron and Joe, they didn't deserve to die! None of this is right!"

He exhales through his nose, raising the gun slightly. "You don't understand the bigger picture. You never will."

I swallow hard. "Then make me understand. What is it all for? Kade, the experiments, what are you and Dr. Heckingbottom even trying to do?"

Blackthorne chuckles dryly. "What we're doing, boy, is evolution. We're pushing the limits of what humanity can become. The world is changing, and we're ensuring we're ahead of it. With an army of people, better than any people can ever dream to be."

My hands tremble, but I press on. "At what cost? How many more people have to die? How many more like Kade will you destroy?"

His expression darkens. "Casualties are necessary.

Progress demands sacrifice."

I shake my head, anger bubbling up past my fear. "That's not progress. That's murder."

Something flickers across his face, just for a second. Doubt? Hesitation? But then it's gone, replaced with cold certainty. He exhales sharply, gripping the gun tighter. "It doesn't matter what you think. You shouldn't have been digging into things you don't understand."

My chest rises and falls in quick, shallow breaths. My fingers tighten around the knife. "I don't want to die..." My voice shakes. "I just want this to stop."

Blackthorne lets out a long sigh, tapping the gun against his temple as if considering. "If I let you go, you'll keep fighting. I can't have that."

A sob escapes me. My legs feel weak, my entire body trembling. "Please... I just—"

And then, something shifts inside me, a courage I never knew I had. I move. I lunge, swinging my fist into Blackthorne's face. My knife flashes toward his side about to cut into him, but—

A deafening bang rings around the room. A white-hot pain tears through my chest. The force knocks me backward, my legs giving out. I hit the floor hard, gasping as warmth pools beneath me. I can't breathe. My fingers press against my chest, but there's too much blood. The door slams shut, his footsteps retreat. He's gone.

I cough, choking as pain rips through me. My chest burns. Each breath is a struggle, sharp and ragged. Cold creeps in fast, spreading through my limbs.

Memories flood my mind as I struggle to stay alive and fight through the pain. Kade, laughing at our dumb jokes. Sneaking out, exploring the city at night, thinking we were invincible. Aaron and Joe. Before it all went wrong. Their voices, their smiles. The way we stood together, believing we could make a difference. My Mum. Her warm hugs. Her soft voice telling me everything would be okay. The search for Kade. The nights spent chasing shadows, fighting despite the fear. Tears slip down my cheeks. I don't want to die. Not like this. Not alone.

My chest shudders. My heartbeat slows. My breath rattles, my fingers twitching as if reaching for something, anything.

I try but darkness creeps in. My vision narrows and my body feels light. My eyes flutter shut and I'm gone, into a dark abyss.

THIRTY-EIGHT
Marlon

We've got a report of a gunshot echoing through Blackwood Forest. Caller didn't see anyone, but they swear something's out there.

- **Report sent to Hearthwick Police Station — Sunday, 20th April 2025**

Dante's bleeding has started to slow down. Luckily the beast hasn't come out of cover to get us yet. It's smart, smarter than I'd given it credit for. It must have some sort of brilliant hunting instinct. We've been hiding here for around twenty minutes without a sight of it, other than the occasional snapping of branches and glistening from its eyes as it circles the ruins. The ruins around us, however, offer little cover, just jagged bits of stone and the remains of something long forgotten.

Through the quiet forest a sharp sound echoes out, scaring some nearby birds, sending them fluttering off into the night. It's a sound I am becoming all too familiar with. A gunshot, loud and clear, not too far away either.

"That's the direction that Duncan ran." mutters Dante, spitting as he speaks, gripping his shoulder tightly.

"We have to go, he might be in trouble." I reply.

Dante sits up and starts scoping out the surroundings.

212

"I haven't heard it in a few minutes, maybe it's gone."

I chuckle, "We'd be so lucky."

I stand and give Dante a hand up with my left hand, my right gripping the pistol loaded with the silver bullet. "Alright, let's go."

We start to make a move, Dante joining me in hobbling a little after his earlier fall. We are careful not to trip as we push through the underbrush. We're moving cautiously and as quietly as we can, scanning for the beast. Something tells me it's still nearby.

Some twigs snap next to us, quick and sharp. I turn and aim my gun, ready to shoot. It's just a wild rabbit, hopping as we pass.

"Fuck me, that scared the hell out of me." I whisper.

Dante giggles. "You big scaredy cat. You get scared over everything, always have bro."

Our laughter is short lived as a shadow shoots in front of us, darting behind a bush. Me and Dante stop in our tracks, quickly getting back to back so that we don't get attacked from behind. I can see Dante is holding his knife tightly, not letting it go. Sweat is pouring from my head as we spin around, trying to locate the creature. I feel dizzy and disorientated.

Dante shouts as it emerges from the shadow, a blur of movement before it fully takes shape. It charges toward us with frightening speed, faster than anything its size should be. We barely have time to react before it slams into us, sending both of us flying like ragdolls. My back smashes into one of the towering oak trees a few meters away; the same spot I hit during the bear attack. The pain flares instantly, a white-hot burst that radiates through my ribs and down my side. It's like the old injury never had a chance to heal. I crumple to the ground, gasping. All the wind is ripped from my lungs, and for a terrifying moment, I can't breathe. Just the sound of pounding

213

footsteps and Dante yelling fills my ears as I struggle to suck in air through the sharp, stabbing ache in my chest.

Dante isn't as lucky as me with his landing, as he's groaning on the floor badly. The beast is looming over him, growling with its teeth shown.

I try to pull myself up but the pain chains me to the tree. I can't help but sit there, watching the beast as he's preparing for the kill. I reach for the gun and raise it. If I can't move my legs, I can at least move my arms. I reach for the pistol that's fallen beside me and raise it, setting sights on the beast. I steady my shaking hand and pull the trigger. The silver bullet finds its target. It buries itself deep into the creature's back. A horrible, ear-splitting howl echoes through the trees as the creature cries out in pain. The beast staggers forward, its claws scrabbling against the ground as its strength falters.

I feel my breath coming back and I attempt to lift myself again. This time succeeding, but with great pain and discomfort. I pull the small vial out of my pocket and move over to the beast. I screw it open and use my fingers to pry open the werewolf's jaw, its teeth snapping weakly with a soft, desperate hiss, as though even in its sedated state, the creature's primal rage still fights to break free. The sharp stench of fur and blood fills the air as its chest heaves with strained breaths, and I feel the tremor in its muscles, a futile reminder of the beast's lingering power. I pour the potion down its throat, forcing its muzzle shut. Its body convulses, its growls turning into strangled gurgles.

Dante tries desperately to get back to his feet. He struggles so I offer him a hand up.

"How long will it take to see if it worked?" He asks.

I shake my head "I'm not sure, I can't remember what the website said. It's best if one of us stays here. If Kade wakes up, he's going to need one of us here. We don't know what state he'll be in."

"Who's gonna go?" Dante asks.

I look at him, he's battered and bruised worse than me. "Absolutely no chance you're going. You can hardly walk, your shoulder is all busted up. I'm going to find Duncan. And then we're getting the hell out of here."

"You're not doing too much better yourself. That's two supernatural attacks on you, and you're still not as injured as me." He chuckles.

I load the pistol with a normal magazine. I can see Dante shaking his head so I say "This isn't gonna be up for a debate bro, I'm going." His face is pale.

The werewolf is still twitching slightly, his whole body jittering every few seconds. There's some small white bits of foam oozing out from the edges of its mouth.

I turn and force myself toward the gunshot, stumbling with every step. My side screams with each movement, but I grit my teeth and keep going. I can't stop now. Hopefully, I'm not too late.

THIRTY-NINE
Marlon

It's hard to locate the gunshot. I know the rough area but the thick vegetation is forming an impenetrable barrier, blocking me from seeing it. A small mist has started to form in the forest, creating a carpet as I move through it.

I start to increase my speed and move through with a much more hurried precision. I need a sign, a light, some movement, anything.

"Duncan!" I shout, cupping both of my hands to my mouth trying to bellow out the noise.

There's no reply. I stand, turning in a circle, hoping to see something. I feel like the forest is swallowing me whole. But then, a flicker. It was only small, but I noticed it. A small light source, that turned on then off again. It must only be about a hundred meters ahead. I start running.

Emerging from the bushes is an old wooden cabin; alone and abandoned. It's covered in vines and overgrown vegetation. I can only think this looks like something out of a horror movie. I notice an old red pickup truck stashed near one of the bushes next to me, partly covered by some overhanging branches.

Gripping the pistol tightly in my hands, I start moving towards the front door. There's a rotten wooden decking in front of the door, the fence surrounding it barely forming a full structure. I'm going in, I've got to. Duncan could be here, trapped, alone.

I step onto the deckings, the wood screaming beneath my feet as it bows down, nearly breaking with my weight. I pull my sleeve over my palm and use it to rub some dust off the window to the left of the front door. All I do is smudge it, creating an opaque glass effect. I put my face to it, looking to see if I can make out any shapes or anything moving.

A noise comes from the other side of the front door, so I lightly step over, making sure that the wood doesn't creak as I step. I'm not careful enough, and as I take my last step, the wood cries out.

I look up, but get sent back, flying with a force that feels unhuman. I don't have time to react as the door gets taken off its hinges and flies with me. I grip onto the sides, hoping it'll give me some sort of protection. I land with a thud and roll backwards, letting go of the door momentarily. I look up and see it. The thing that threw me back like a ragdoll. An old face that's haunted me for weeks. It's real, it's the bear.

The bear lunges at me with a swiping paw, but I manage to grab the door just in time, lifting it to take the blow like a makeshift shield. The impact makes me wince and take a step back to soften the impact. Four massive scratch imprints decorate the door as I try to use it to fend it off. The bear stands on its back legs, towering at least five feet taller than me. Gritting my teeth, I throw the door forward in an attempt to distract the beast so I can make a break for it. The bear takes half a step back as the door lands in front of him. I use the half a second hesitation as my chance to make a break for the cabin, the best cover I can see.

The bear runs towards me, trying to stop me reaching it. I turn and unload three shots into him. The shots embed themselves into the monster, but they only do as much as make

217

him flinch. How can I kill this thing? It's the same creature that killed Churchill.

I lunge through the entrance with great pain, slamming a storage dresser into the doorframe in a useless attempt to slow my pursuer. There's a few other wooden pieces of furniture which I carelessly throw to the doorway.

My eyes dart across the dim room until they land on a jerry can tucked against the wall. Snatching it up, I twist off the cap and start pouring fuel across the wooden floor as I rush towards the stairs. Behind me, I hear the bear tearing through the doorway. Its claws scrape against the floorboards, each step heavier than the last. I bound up the stairs two at a time even though my body protests it, tossing whatever I can find from the top. Chairs, an old TV and a wooden crate are amongst the many things I throw down the steps in a desperate attempt to slow the beast. I continue to pour the fuel. The smell stinging my nostrils.

I run into one of the rooms upstairs and nearly trip over a body. It's Duncan. I drop to one knee and cover my mouth with shock. I roll him onto his back, hoping for a sign of life. No pulse. His lifeless eyes stare at the ceiling, his body coated in thick, red blood. A sharp pain shoots through my chest, grief and fury twisting together. How could I let this happen, how could I let him go.

A guttural roar snaps me back to reality. I look up through my sobbing eyes and see the outline of the bear reach the top of the stairs, pushing through the last of the makeshift barricade. This is it, this is personal. First it was Churchill, then Antonio, then Joe and Aaron, and now Duncan. Whether it's the bear, Dr Blackthorne or someone else, I'm gonna take you all down. I throw the jerry can around, splashing the last remnants of fuel around upstairs. I stand up straight, pulling out the lighter that Dante gave to me. The bear turns the corner of the stairs and looks at me dead in the eyes. I flick the lighter open, a small flame emerges and I throw it forward into the fuel-soaked floor.

The fire catches immediately, spreading like a living thing. The beast's growls turn into a snarl of rage as flames lick at its fur, but it doesn't stop. It charges through the fire, its body partly ablaze. Smoke starts to billow around me, stinging my eyes, burning my throat and seeping into my open wounds all over my body. I stumble back, coughing violently, as the floor beneath me groans in protest.

The bear swipes at me, its claws carving through the air. I jump backwards, narrowly avoiding it. The floor creaks under the bear and starts to give way. I clamber over the bed and dive back through the doorway into the landing as the bear nearly falls through the room, its upper body clawing at the edge.

I hold my arm up to my mouth to cover some of the smoke that's trying to engulf me. I won't wait. With every ounce of strength, I grab a shattered beam and ram it into the bear's exposed chest. It howls in agony, flames crawling up its fur. The bear, now enraged, claws back onto the second floor and swings another paw at me. This time I dodge left, grabbing a splintered piece of wood from the collapsing wall and driving it into the creature's smoldering shoulder. It roars in pain as I grunt, but still, it presses forward. I swing wildly, using the broken wood like a crude club, smashing it against the bear's skull. It doesn't act affected by it.

The bear lets out a guttural roar and swings a massive claw at me. It slashes across my shoulder, and agony explodes through my body. I cry out, stumbling back as warm blood gushes down my arm. The force of the blow nearly knocks me off my feet, and the world spins for a second as I fight to stay upright. Then it lunges in, jaws wide, teeth gleaming.

219

Panicking, I fumble for my pistol with my off-hand. My dominant one feels useless, numb from the wound. I fire blindly into its mouth. The shots echo like thunder, and I keep pulling the trigger, emptying the magazine as fast as I can. The beast jerks, snarls, but doesn't fall. I pull the trigger again, this time it's empty.

The bear is still standing. It looms over me, blood mixing with the froth at its mouth, eyes burning with fury. I can see the bullet wounds in its gums and tongue, but it doesn't slow. Bullets don't kill it. No matter how many I fire, it keeps coming. And now I've got nothing left.

The thick smoke makes me cough, and I start to feel dizzy. I quickly glance behind me, and even though my sight is limited, I can make out a window a few meters behind me at the end of the landing. I turn, moving as quickly as my body lets me, pain trying to pull me down. I move through the thickening smoke and hurl myself through the glass. The world blurs as I crash through, shards slicing my arms before I hit the ground with a bone-rattling thud.

Gasping, I roll onto my back. I wipe away some soot that had gotten into my eyes as I struggle to pull air into my lungs, but then I hear it. The sickening crack of wood breaking behind me. I turn to see it. It's the bear.

As I crawl backwards, It leaps through the flames, landing in the dirt, its body still burning. Smoke curls from its fur, its eyes filled with unrelenting rage. It steps forward, towering over me, fire licking at its form. I can barely move; No bullets, no weapons. The bear's drooling mouth is just above my head. It's going to finish me off.

FORTY
Kade

The Lycantheum Elixir, a rare concoction born of moonlit herbs and ancient alchemy, promises to mend the cursed flesh of the lycanthrope and restore the man to his true form. One drink, and the beast shall slumber, the claws and fangs fading into memory. But beware—should you attempt to heal the cursed during the full moon, the Elixir's power will falter. It cannot fully mend what the moon has already corrupted, and the transformation will resist. The curse, though momentarily tempered, shall remain unbroken, and the Elixir can never again restore the balance. Once consumed in such a state, the potion will be forever impotent, and the wolf will never fully vanish.

- *Elias Blackthorne, Veteran Monster Hunter, 1461 AD*

The first thing I feel is the cold. It creeps through my skin, wrapping around my bones. The next thing is pain. Deep, raw, like my muscles have been torn apart and stitched back together wrong. My head throbs, my thoughts sluggish and disconnected. I force my eyes open, blinking against the dim light filtering through the trees.

The forest stretches around me, dark and endless. The towering trees loom over me, their branches clawing at the sky.

Moonlight filters through the canopy, casting long, shifting shadows over the damp earth. The quiet is unnerving. Too empty. Too unfamiliar.

Panic grips my chest. Where am I? How did I get here? The last thing I remember is the lab. Carl and I were trying to escape. We were trying to find a way out, and then... darkness.

My hands tremble as I push myself upright. My clothes are shredded, my skin smeared with dirt and dried blood. I stare at my hands, human hands. But something feels wrong. My body isn't mine. It's exhausted, sore in ways that don't make sense.

A groan draws my attention, and I turn sharply. A man is slumped against a fallen tree a few feet away, clutching his shoulder. He looks like he's been through hell, battered and bruised, his breathing unsteady. He's older than me, mid-to-late twenties maybe, with dark hair and a sharp gaze that flickers with something between exhaustion and relief as he looks at me.

"You're back," he mutters, exhaling like a weight has been lifted.

I stiffen. "Who—who are you?"

The relief in his expression fades slightly. "Dante."

That name means nothing to me. My pulse quickens. "Why are you here? How do you know me?"

Dante winces as he shifts. "It's a long story. You had changed into something else. But right now, we have a problem." He hesitates, then sighs. "Duncan ran off."

My stomach drops. "What?"

Dante grimaces. "He saw everything. He panicked."

I barely hear the rest. My chest tightens, and suddenly, I can't breathe. I think of his dumb jokes, his nervous smile, the way he looked up to me like I was some kind of big brother at times. And now he's out there, alone, scared, because of me.

222

"Marlon's gone after him, I heard a few gunshots a minute ago," Dante adds, but I barely register it. I don't know that name either.

I push myself to my feet too fast, the world tilting. I brace a hand against the tree, forcing myself to stay upright. "I—I need to help," I say, though my body protests with every movement.

Dante eyes me warily. "You barely know where you are right now. You need a minute to process everything."

"I don't have a minute," I snap. I don't know Dante. I don't know how I got here. But I do know Duncan, and if he's in trouble, I'm not standing around waiting. Whatever happened to me, whatever I became, I have to figure it out later. Right now, I have to move.

Something catches my gaze as I go to say something to Dante. Something bright, burning. It stands out like a sore thumb.

"What's that?" I point.

Dante pulls himself to his feet and turns. "Oh no, that's the way Marlon ran."

We don't exchange words, just exchange a short glance at each other before turning and running to the fire. Running feels weird, like it's a foreign movement.

The cold night air burns in my lungs as I run, my legs ache with exhaustion. Dante stumbles beside me, limping heavily, each step punctuated with a sharp inhale of pain. The distant glow of fire flickers through the thick forest, a violent contrast against the dark. The scent of smoke sharpens in my nose, mixed with something else, something musky and wild. My heart pounds harder.

We burst through the last tangle of branches and into a clearing. The cabin is engulfed in flames, embers spiraling into the night sky like dying stars. The heat presses against my skin, but my eyes are locked on the figure lying on the ground. I don't recognise the face but this must be Marlon. His body is sprawled on the floor, almost motionless.

A massive shape looms over him. A bear bigger than I've ever seen. Its dark fur gleams with sweat and blood, breath coming in ragged huffs as it closes in for the kill. Its teeth glisten in the firelight, claws digging into the dirt, preparing to strike.

I freeze. A sickening weight settles in my gut, pressing me down, keeping me still. My limbs shake, not from exhaustion but from fear. The image of the bear ripping into Marlon flashes through my mind, but my feet won't move. My body won't listen.

Dante grabs my arm, his voice raw. "Kade, get out of here, it's too dangerous!"

I panic, I feel helpless. It all surges inside me, clawing at my chest. I squeeze my eyes shut, willing it away, but it only grows stronger. A heat builds beneath my skin, boiling, surging through my veins like liquid fire. My breath shudders. My muscles twitch.

"No, no, no… what's happening?" I cry out.

Dante looks at me speechless as I gasp, doubling over as my bones crack like snapping branches. My hands slam into the dirt, fingers stretching, nails splitting as they darken and lengthen into claws. Fire rips through my spine, forcing me onto all fours as my limbs stretch and reshape. My already shredded clothes tighten as my body expands, muscle piling onto muscle. My face burns, skull shifting, mouth stretching into a snout filled with razor-sharp teeth. I throw my head back and scream, but what comes out is a deep, guttural snarl.

Dante stumbles back, his voice shaking. "That cure… It was supposed to stop this!"

I suck in a breath, scenting everything at once. The

fire, the blood, the bear, my mind is a storm, thoughts tangled in rage, instinct screaming for violence. I feel the anger, the urge to rip and tear, but I can still think. I can still recognize faces. I can't remember anything from before. Dante said I changed, was it into this? If it was then why am I still changing? He said he gave me a cure.

The bear stares at me and rears back, ready to strike. A growl rumbles from my chest, deep and raw. I don't want to be this thing, but I have to use these powers to save this helpless man. My claws dig into the earth. The anger swells inside me, I don't fight it though. I'm going to use it.

The bear meets me head-on, its massive claws swinging through the air. I duck, feeling the wind rush over my fur as its swipe narrowly misses my skull. I slam into its chest, knocking it back, but it barely stumbles before roaring and surging forward again.

We collide, teeth and claws tearing into each other. Pain sears through my shoulder as the bear's fangs sink in, but I barely register it. I lash out, raking my claws across its face, feeling flesh and fur tear beneath my grip. The bear howls and swings a paw into my ribs, sending me crashing into the dirt.

Dante rushes in as quickly as he can, grabbing a burning log from the ground. He swings it like a bat, striking the bear's side. It snarls, momentarily distracted, and Marlon takes his chance. He stumbles to his feet, picking up a jagged piece of wood, and drives it into the bear's hind leg. The beast roars in fury and pain, twisting violently.

I push myself up, my vision red with rage. I pounce, sinking my fangs into its neck. We thrash, rolling across the clearing, the firelight casting monstrous shadows on the trees. Blood splatters onto the dirt. The bear grips my side and throws me off, sending me crashing into a tree. I shake my head, clearing the stars from my vision. The beast is limping now,

225

injured but still dangerous.

Marlon spots movement near the burning cabin. "Blackthorne!"

A man emerges from the flames, coughing, clutching a glass vial in one hand and a folder filled with documents in the other. He spots us fighting and doesn't hesitate. He runs towards an old red pickup truck hidden under overhanging branches. Marlon staggers after him, but he's too slow. Blackthorne jumps in, starts the engine, and peels away, disappearing into the forest before Marlon can reach him.

Marlon curses, turning back just in time to see the bear lunge for me again.

I snarl and dart forward, my claws sinking deep into its chest. The beast roars, but I push forward, using all my strength to drive us both toward a nearby tree. Its back slams into a thick, broken branch, and with a sickening crunch, the wood spears through its body.

The bear shudders; its roars turning into wet, gasping breaths. It twitches, then slowly slumps. The monstrous shape trembles, then begins to shrink.

I step back, panting. I feel my body start to change again. This time my muscles are shrinking down. I fall to one knee as I'm off-balance. I'm turning back into myself again.

I look up to watch as the bear's fur recedes, claws retract, and its massive form twists and contracts. Within moments, a human body lies impaled on the branch, motionless. Blood seeps into the ground. I take a step closer to see who it is. Recognition slams into me like a freight train. I know this man.

"The Brute..." I murmur, my voice barely more than a growl. I saw him in the lab, locked away, just like I was. Though he wanted to be there, intimidating me like a bully. I don't know who else is out there. What curses they possess.

226

What horrors they've been through.

FORTY-ONE
Marlon

The flickering orange glow of the burning cabin dances across the trees, casting long shadows. Smoke curls into the night sky, thick and acrid, stinging my eyes as I struggle to stay on my feet. My body aches, every bit of movement sends fresh waves of pain through me. Blood trickles from a gash above my eye, but I barely register it. My focus is on Kade.

He kneels in the dirt, his bare skin streaked with soot and sweat, his breath ragged. The last remnants of the fight still linger in his trembling limbs. His hands clutch at his head, his fingers digging into his scalp as if trying to block out the truth I have to tell him.

"Duncan's dead."

The words hang in the air like a death sentence. For a moment, there's silence. Then, his breath hitches, his whole body stiffening before he lets out a broken sob. His shoulders shake violently as grief crashes into him, raw and unforgiving. I watch as he crumbles, his hands clawing at the dirt as if trying to ground himself, but there's no escape from this.

"No... No, no, no—" he gasps, his voice cracking as he shakes his head wildly. "He—he can't be. I—" He grips his chest as if his heart might shatter apart, and I feel like the worst person alive for having to say it.

I crouch beside him. I wince as I place a hand on

Kade's shoulder. "I'm sorry, kid," I say, my voice hoarse. "I... I found him upstairs in the cabin. There's nothing I could do. He didn't make it."

Kade's howl of anguish cuts through the night, more inhuman than anything he sounded like in his wolf form. The fire crackles behind us, but its heat is nothing compared to the torment burning in his eyes as he looks at me. His face is twisted in grief, but there's something else too... guilt.

"I was a monster. The only thing I can remember since the lab was that fight just now. I think I'm losing my mind."

Dante replies, "We gave you a cure, well... I guess it didn't fully work. Like you're in control now, but it hasn't fully healed you."

"The cure... it didn't stop me from turning," he whispers, his voice shaking. "Why? Why didn't it work?"

I swallow hard. I don't have an answer, and that terrifies me. I exhale, forcing myself to steady my voice. "You're not a monster," I say firmly. "But until you get this fully under control... I get why you're scared."

Before he can respond, a new light cuts through the darkness. Flashing red and blue, weaving through the trees. The sound of tires crunching over dirt reaches us, then the distant murmur of voices. It's the police.

Kade's head snaps up, his tear-streaked face hardening in an instant. He stares at the approaching lights, his body tensing as if ready to run.

"I can't be here," he says suddenly, voice tight with fear. "I won't... I can't let them take me. I won't be a lab rat again."

"Kade—" Dante starts, but he's already moving.

He stumbles to his feet, his body still weak from the fight, but determination drives him forward. With one last glance at me and Dante, he turns and bolts into the trees,

229

disappearing into the shadows. I watch him go, jaw clenched, but I don't call out. I understand. If I were in his position, I'd run too.

A moment later, the police cars pull up, their headlights cutting harsh beams through the smoke. Officers step out, weapons lowered but ready. They look at me and Dante, eyes flicking to our bloodied clothes, wrecked bodies, and the burning wreckage behind us.

Dante sighs, rubbing a hand over his face. "Well, this is going to be fun."

I force myself to straighten up, ignoring the pain screaming through my body. "We don't have a choice," I mutter. "We have to tell them."

Dante grunts, clearly not happy about it. "Yeah. Doesn't mean I trust 'em. We already know that Langford girl you were on about is one of them. We don't even know who else is in this."

"Neither do I, and I have no idea, but we're about to find out." I glance at the fire, at the destruction left in its wake. My fists tighten. We've lost too much; Duncan, Churchill, Kade's peace of mind, and Blackthorne is still out there, with whatever was in that vial.

I turn my gaze back to the officers, steel settling in my bones. This isn't over, not until every last one of them pays for what they've done.

FORTY-TWO
Kade

I trudge through the forest, the moonlight fading fast as the first light of morning creeps in. I've been running for hours. My breath comes in sharp, desperate gasps, curling in the cold air like smoke. My clothes are shredded, barely clinging to my filthy skin, and every inch of me still aches from the transformation.

I scramble over a fallen log and spot a small, shadowy cave tucked beneath a cluster of trees. Without thinking, I collapse at the entrance, chest heaving. I stare at my shaking hands, trying to pull myself together, trying to breathe. The morning sun begins to break through the treetops, forcing me to shield my eyes.

"Need to be away from people," I whisper, choking back a sob. "Why did this happen to me?"

To the left of the cave entrance, I hear it; a stream, gentle and steady. I turn my head and see the water flowing peacefully, a few tiny fish drifting along like nothing's wrong. It's almost laughable. That calm serenity, so out of place after all the blood and chaos.

My veins still feel like they're on fire. I crawl to the edge of the stream and plunge my hands in, trying to wash away the last of the wolf. The icy water climbs up my arms as I

231

splash it onto my face. Dirt, soot, dried blood; it all starts to run off, carried away by the current. I lean over the water and catch my reflection. I see me, but it's not me. Not the cheeky, rebellious kid I used to be. There's a monster staring back, hiding just beneath my skin. The cure didn't work. Duncan's dead because of it. Because of me.

My hands curl into fists, fingernails digging into my palms. My jaw locks up as I fight back the surge of emotion. I can't go back. Not yet.

Suddenly, I hear a noise from inside the cave. Some rocks shift and something moves. I freeze.

"Who's there?" I call out, tense, my body ready to snap.

A figure steps from the shadows and into the pale light. It's a woman. She looks scared, but there's something strange about her. Her clothes are torn and streaked with soot, one sleeve barely hanging on. Her face is smeared with dirt and dried blood, a fresh cut still raw above her brow. Her eyes dart around, wild and glassy, like someone who's seen too much, run too far, and is still waiting for the next horror to strike. She limps slightly as she moves, every step cautious, like the ground itself might betray her.

"Back off! Look, just leave me alone. I don't want any trouble," she shouts, her voice sharp with fear, the lilt of an Italian accent breaking through.

I blink, stunned. How is someone here? This deep in the woods?

"I don't want trouble either," I say carefully. "I'm just trying to get away from everything. I should go. I'm not safe to be around."

"Wait!" she cries out, stepping closer. "I think I know you."

I frown. "What?"

232

"You used to come into my shop, I'm sure of it," she says, eyes wide with realisation.

"What's your name?" I ask, wary.

"Sophia. My husband Antonio and I ran the pizza shop. I escaped that sick bastard when the cabin caught fire. I jumped out the back window and ran... ran until I couldn't run anymore."

FORTY-THREE

The house was still. The only sound was the hum of the fridge in the corner of the kitchen, the steady beat of life that somehow, impossibly, went on. Cynthia stood by the counter, hands clasped around a half-empty cup of tea that had long since gone cold. Her eyes were unfocused, staring out the window at the grey morning sky, waiting for something. Anything.

The night had been quiet, too quiet, and she couldn't shake the feeling that something wasn't right. Duncan hadn't called, hadn't checked in. He always checked in.

She told herself it was nothing, they probably didn't have any signal. That they were probably too caught up in his investigation, or lost in his own thoughts, like he often was. But as the hours ticked by, the silence grew heavier. Pressing against her chest, suffocating her.

Then the phone rang. It was loud, jarring, shattering the silence in the way only a phone call could. Cynthia's heart skipped, a heavy lump forming in her throat as she reached for the receiver. Her hand trembled, just a little.

"Hello?"

The voice on the other end was muffled at first, distant. She couldn't make out the words. And then, then it hit her. It was a voice she didn't recognize.

"Ma'am, are you Miss. Cynthia Webb?"

234

She gripped the phone harder, the world around her narrowing as the name tumbled out, like the air was being sucked from the room. "Yes... Yes, that's me."

There was a pause, long enough to let her nerves twist and curl around her insides. And then the words came. Words that she could never have prepared enough for, no matter how many times she imagined the worst case scenario.

"I'm so sorry, ma'am. It's... it's about your son, Duncan. He... he's gone. He passed away in the woods. We... we found him, but we couldn't get to him in time."

Her breath caught, the world tilting sideways. The phone slipped from her ear, hanging in mid-air, a faint static buzz filling her mind. She didn't hear the rest of what was said. She couldn't.

The cup of tea dropped from her hands, shattering on the floor with a loud smash. She couldn't focus on that. Couldn't focus on anything except the cold, numbing shock that was slowly, steadily overtaking her. Her son. Her baby boy. The boy who had always been so full of life, so determined to find answers, to make the world better. He had been strong, so strong. He had been everything to her. And now... now he was gone.

Cynthia collapsed onto the floor, her knees giving out as the world closed in around her, barely giving a care for the chips of the mug scattered along the floor. Her hands trembled as they pressed to her face, trying to stifle the sobs that racked her body. Her chest burned, as if her heart had been ripped out and replaced with something too raw, too jagged to bear.

This wasn't real. This couldn't be real. She had imagined a thousand things, things she feared could happen, things she couldn't stop, things she knew would one day come. But nothing, nothing had prepared her for this. For the finality of it. For the emptiness that now swallowed her whole.

She tried to speak, tried to say something, anything, but her voice was lost, drowned by the overwhelming weight of grief. Her body shook violently, her breaths shallow, quick. She could feel herself breaking in ways she never thought possible.

"Duncan," she whispered hoarsely, the word a jagged gasp that tore through her throat. "My boy…"

In that moment, she wasn't alone. Latisha was kneeling beside her, her arms around Cynthia's shaking shoulders, her voice gentle, soothing. "I'm here, Cynthia. I'm here. I know it's hard, but you're not alone. You're not alone."

Kyle stood a few feet away in the kitchen, his head buried in his hands, his posture hunched with the weight of his own grief. The space between them felt vast, the air thick with sorrow. He had been with them all, shared the same fear for Duncan's safety. And now… now, they were all left to pick up the pieces.

But Latisha, steady and strong, never let go of Cynthia. Her fingers stroked through Cynthia's hair, a quiet comfort, a reminder that there was still a thread of connection. Still something to hold onto, even if the world had come crashing down.

Cynthia couldn't speak, couldn't move. The world around her was a blur of pain and disbelief. She clung to Latisha, the warmth of the embrace offering a shred of solace in the face of overwhelming loss. Her son. Her Duncan.

"I should've—" Cynthia's voice cracked as she tried to speak, but the words wouldn't come, suffocated by her grief. "I should've been there. I should've protected him."

Latisha shook her head, her voice steady. "You can't blame yourself. You loved him. You always did everything you could. This isn't on you."

Cynthia could only nod, her body trembling as the tears flowed freely, as the weight of her loss settled deep into

236

her bones. It felt like the earth itself had shifted beneath her, leaving her stranded on an island of grief.

And in that silence, as the sobs racked her body, the world outside seemed distant, unreachable. Everything that once mattered felt meaningless now. Cynthia's baby boy was gone. And she didn't know how to live without him.

EPILOGUE 1: NO REST FOR THE STRONG

Carl stands at the edge of the rooftop, the wind tugging at his jacket as he stares down at the streets below. The city at night is alive, a restless beast of flickering neon, distant sirens, and the low hum of engines rolling over wet asphalt. The streetlights stretch out in endless rows, glowing like artificial stars against the deep indigo of the sky. A fine mist lingers in the air, carrying the scent of rain and exhaust fumes.

From his vantage point, he watches the world move. Cars slow at intersections, their headlights cutting through the darkness in stark white beams. A bus rumbles past, passengers lost in their own thoughts, unaware of the man standing above them, balancing between past and future. Pedestrians move like ghosts along the pavement, some hurrying to escape the chill, others lost in conversation. It all feels so normal. Too normal for a world that he knows is anything but.

Then he sees it; a figure in a dark hoodie and a cheap plastic mask darting toward a woman near a convenience store. The flicker of a knife catches the light as the masked man lunges, his voice lost to the city's noise but his intent clear. The woman recoils, hands clutching her bag, terror written in her every movement.

Carl exhales slowly. He's spent too long running, too

long hiding in the shadows, waiting for the fight to come to him. But not tonight.

"No more running," he mutters under his breath.

A faint, familiar crackle stirs at his fingertips. Tiny arcs of electricity dance between his knuckles, illuminating his clenched fists with flickering light. The air around him hums with static, a charge building in the space between heartbeats.

EPILOGUE 2: THE NEXT MOVE

A lone figure stands in a high-rise office, silhouetted against the sprawling London skyline. The city glows beneath him, streetlights stretching like veins through the urban sprawl, headlights weaving between them like restless fireflies. From this height, the world looks small. Insignificant.

His long, black coat drapes over his frame, shifting slightly as he moves. His dark hair, parted cleanly, falls past his ears, framing a face too sharp, too perfect, preserved by something beyond time. He taps a gloved hand against his leg as he strides toward a sleek mahogany desk. Without hesitation, he lifts the phone and dials.

The line clicks. A voice answers.

"Heckingbottom," the man murmurs, his voice smooth yet carrying an edge of quiet menace. "I heard what happened at Lab Theta. People are going to start asking questions."

A brief pause, then Heckingbottom's voice comes through, laced with strained composure. "It's being handled. Blackthorne managed to recover one of the vials."

The figure's fingers tighten slightly around the receiver. "And the test subjects?"

"They mostly died in the blaze, Sophia slipped out when the place was alight. Carl was a bit before but we're closing in on him. As for the other one, we're working to find him," Heckingbottom replies, a flicker of unease in his tone.

The figure exhales slowly, his gloved fingers tracing his jawline, a sharp, calculated gesture. "I'm aware these aren't the only subjects you've let slip through your fingers. There was a breach at Lab Gamma as well. A woman. And from what I hear, she's powerful."

A longer pause. Then, more carefully: "Understood. We'll tie up our loose ends."

The figure's lips curve into something that isn't quite a smile. "See that you do." He leans back slightly, glancing at the city below. "Actually, don't worry, I'm going to send someone to clean up the mess. Just make sure your cover isn't compromised. Chimera must remain intact, and our peoples' positions across the area remain. It is vital to the plan."

Before Heckingbottom can respond, the figure ends the call with a quiet click. He turns, his movements slow, deliberate. Each step echoes against the polished floor. This isn't the end; merely the beginning.

ABOUT THE AUTHOR

William Lee is a writer with a passion for flawed heroes, dark conspiracies, and the kind of buried truths that refuse to stay hidden. *Gone Before the Moon* is his debut novel, and the first in a planned series set in a modern world where superhuman powers are emerging; alongside a creeping darkness.

Inspired by a wide range of comics, TV shows, and films that explore superheroes, the supernatural, and unsolved mysteries, William brings a cinematic energy and emotional grit to his storytelling.

When he's not writing, he enjoys playing and watching football, loyally supporting Wolverhampton Wanderers, as well as game nights and all things trivia.

This is just the beginning of his journey. More stories are on the way!

JOIN MY NEWSLETTER

I hope you enjoyed this story! If you would like to keep up to date with my books, aswell as behind the scenes content you can do so here:

Printed in Dunstable, United Kingdom

65940655R00141